THEN COMES A WIND

A Novel

By

R J Stewart

Copyright © 2023 by RJ Stewart
This is a work of fiction. Names, characters, businesses, organizations, places, events, and incidents either are the product of the author's imagination or are used fictitiously. Any resemblance to actual persons, living or dead, events, or locales is entirely coincidental.

All rights reserved.

Published by RJ Stewart

Printed in United States of America

ISBN: 9780996544146

Here comes the little wind which the hour
Drags with it everywhere like an empty wagon through leaves.
- *W. S. Merwin*

For Jay, Elsie,
Velma, and Melva

1

Will

WILL SUTTON pushed his arms through the sleeves of his wool shirt. He walked stiffly to the bare table and looked across it to the dirt wall where a calendar hung on a wooden peg. Twenty-eight days of March 1907 were crossed out, and he found the stubby pencil and marked through the twenty-ninth.

He pulled his felt hat from the peg and went to the steps of the root cellar door. He pushed his head and shoulder upward against its bulky weight. It didn't move. He pushed again using his bent legs, and it gave way. He glanced back to see if Almy or Viola stirred, but they slept soundly pulled together, the straw-filled ticking tucked under their chins. Maddie scowled from the dark room then nodded him away, and he stepped up and out the door of the sod hut.

Behind the iron hinges, sand fell from the door and into its crude frame. More sand fell onto the steps below and into the dugout. Maddie's brow furrowed, disdainful. Dirt. Why didn't he use the porch door?

He lowered the door as gently as he could, and it banged into place. He sniffed the wind coming up and over his back, then he turned against it, to his right, westward, and went down the mound. Air across his shoulder was crisp and gusted into his open shirt. He pulled his chin into his chest. The outhouse was a short walk ahead, the sod barn to his left thirty steps away, downwind from the sod hut. He heard throaty neighs from the horses and the shuffle of their hooves, the swish of their tails.

He stopped short of the outhouse. He spat, loosened his pants, and relieved himself. His water barely puddled, disappeared quickly into the sand. He looked at his track with scorn, piss on sand on land he would own in seven hundred and seventy-six days. Sand where he urinated to him seemed like a moat around each tuft of grass. Each tuft like a day, he thought, five years of days like a lifetime of work and persistence that would pay off only when he could own it outright and sell a small crop or market his growing herd or sell the whole damned entry to the cattlemen.

He turned toward his barn, admiring its earthen walls ten feet high. With borrowed money from his grandfather, Sutton bought wood a year ago for rafters and the loft. Two stalls of sod below kept the horses protected in the winter. He entered through the south-facing opening and wondered when he could afford to hang doors. He reached for the pail to pull the milk from the cow. He balanced on the one-legged stool and soothed the beast while he placed his thumb and index fingers around her teats and massaged the milk down and out, into the pail. The bigger horse was nervous again, made a throaty neigh, stomped its hooves, paced the stall.

He pulled up from the cow and went to the stall. In the corner he saw the snake, a good six feet long, cornering a kangaroo rat. Drawn to the barn for grain, the rat had encountered its arch enemy. Sutton knew the rat's community, a hundred yards away beneath needle-and-thread plants, where many lived, pests to him.

He opened the crude barricade on the stall and freed the horse. Neither the snake nor the rat seemed to notice. The rat turned its long-tailed end to the snake's head and kicked at the hardened barn floor to discourage the snake with dirt to its face. The compacted manure, dirt and sand didn't budge, a failed tactic. The snake advanced. Sutton watched, a territory dispute unfolding before him.

He didn't want to involve himself; the snake with luck might do the job without his help, but he watched with interest. The rat turned to face the predator, and as the snake advanced it leaped instantly three feet into the air, straight up. When it landed the snake snapped forward, wrapping itself in the blink of an eye around the rat and constricting grotesquely.

Sutton watched the snake twist and tighten, and the rat turned upside down, its head invisible in the folds of the snake's tightening length. He saw the large hind legs of the small mammal, the muscles taut in hopeless struggle, the small power that the rat possessed now incapable of pushing. He saw the entrails extrude and imagined with a shudder the feel of the snake's patient power, the rat's ribs snapping, its heart racing and its small mind blanking. He could not see the eyes of the dying rat, and only curiosity compelled him to stare at the guts oozing from it.

In minutes the struggle ceased, and the snake loosened its hold and turned its head to the rat's head, disjointed its jaws and began the long process of eating. The disjointed jaws opened easily to accommodate the breadth of the rat's head. With lunges it advanced its grip and engorged more and more of the rat. At last, only the once-powerful hind legs remained with the mess and the tapered tail, and the snake ate it all.

2

Maddie

SUTTON PAUSED at the shanty door with his milk pail. The weather looked promising this morning. It was two days by wagon to Rackett, and he should put in supplies before spring work mounted. It was nearly a year ago when Maddie and the girls made the last trip with him. Now Easter neared. Little money to buy them, but the supplies were needed. The rising sun pushed the night away. Beyond the barn, bunchgrass waved in the breeze, brightening gold as the sun rose. On the pond, green- winged teal, early in their summer migration, plied the rippling water and dived for mollusks. At the shore, a heron foraged among the reeds. Bunches of yellow-headed blackbirds brushed the water then settled into cattails. He lifted the cellar door and stepped in.

"Whyn't you use the south door, Will? Last thing I need is more dirt."

She looked at his narrow face and large features, a match for his frame. She loved him with all his folly. She told herself often that she was committed to see things through, to stick with it, and to one day own the land. Most of the challenges were manageable, but the dirt and the dust were her enemy. Like a soldier with a broom and a wet cloth for weapons, she patrolled the hut ceaselessly. She held the idea of cleanliness as if it were her best hope for order and control. Sutton awkwardly tried to disarm her.

"Now, Maddie. This here's a nice dirt rug to go over your nice dirt floor."

His smile could melt her when she was angry with him. She said that smile could turn a wolf into a puppy with its warmth and sincerity. She looked at his ample rusty hair parted at a tuft just left of middle, above his shallow brow and thick black eyebrows that grew together. His narrow-set blue eyes were lodged deep in his face, underscored with puffy folds of skin and separated by a prominent nose. It all seemed handsome and resolute to her. His large chin, cleft, seemed to punctuate his toothy smile, like a period at the end of simple sentence. On either cheek were two deep creases, amplified when he laughed, which he often did. His face was complex, unconfined, and capable at once of confidence, assurance, protection, warning and welcome. She was aware, too, that when crossed he could turn fearsome.

Accepting his tease, she gave an unconvincing scowl, expressed with puckered lips and folded arms, in mock defiance. She went back to her work at the stove.

"Well, look who's up and ready for another day. Mornin' girls," he said. They ignored him and sat on the bench at the table.

"If this weather holds, we're going to Rackett tomorrow," he said.

The prospect of a trip to town brightened their faces, especially Maddie's.

"Anybody interested?"

The girls raised their hands quickly and waved enthusiastically. Maddie turned from the stove.

"I'd love to see Charles and Mildred," she said. "Wouldn't it be nice to catch up on the news?

"You think that old inkpot of a brother-in-law of yours knows any goings on? Maddie, sometimes I think he can't keep track of his own legs, let alone the news of this wilderness."

"You hush, Will. Charles knows everyone in this wide-open country. Anyway, I want time with Sis; it's been too long."

"You girls are mighty quiet. No plans for you in Rackett?" Sutton's innocent question assured Almy.

"I'd like to find a book, Pa. Maybe Uncle Charles has found Robinson Crusoe for me."

Almy had no school to show for her twelve years, except what Maddie and Sutton had taught her, but she was quick with words, and read everything she could get her hands on. Little Viola, six, had tried but so far hadn't figured out the strange code. She preferred being outdoors anyway, helping her Pa whenever she could.

Sutton removed his hat and returned it to the peg driven into the dirt wall. He surveyed the squalid shanty that was his family's home and thought of the work he'd put into it, with Maddie's help. Her strength and determination supported his own, but the dirt bedeviled her.

Still, this soddie was theirs, this place on six-hundred and forty acres in western Nebraska. He cut the sod and laid it in with recollection of pictures he saw in books in St. Louis before he came west. Most of the neighbors made their walls straight up, but Sutton made the lower rows wide on the outside perimeter, and tapered them as they rose, finally to nine feet and almost two feet thick at the top.

He dug his shanty deep into a south-facing hill and opened its front door to the south, out to the barn and the wide prairie. His home, half sod hut and half dugout, would endure at least for the five years they needed to prove up. Two winters now had thrown all they had at him, he thought, but by god the hut was warm and the good earth hid them from wind and snow and hot summer sun.

Sutton carried the days in his head; nine-hundred and eighty-eight days had passed since he filed on July 13, 1904. Two summers and two winters remained until their Kincaid entry -- his homestead -- would be his. He knew he could last, and Maddie could, too, if the dirt would let her alone. He thought the next project should be to price some rough lumber in Rackett and lay a wooden floor, maybe this summer.

Sutton said, "We'll hitch the team in the morning. Maddie, pack some extra bedding in case it storms. I'm countin' on the Jensens puttin' us up for the night. Those Danes are the kindest people in the world. I wouldn't trade one of them for all the damned Deasts in the world."

"Will! That's enough."

Maddie didn't like the slur and she surely didn't like the profanity. Deast meant nothing to the girls, except what she and Sutton implied with the unnecessary offhand comments. Too much weight on small shoulders can press a small heart into hardness. She saw no reason to trouble them. They could know about those things in adulthood, when trouble, like time, was unavoidable.

"You girls finish up and get to chores," she said.

Her hair was pulled tight on her head and held with combs. A few years ago her hair was lighter but now, at thirty years old, her hair was the color of the worn and rusting plowshares Sutton stacked near the barn. Bathing was intermittent, limited to cloth washes during the cold winter months, and then dependent upon a sufficient supply of chips to heat water from the shallow well. Soon the summer breeze and high sun would make bathing easier and far more enjoyable, when she and the girls could wash in the pond and laze in the summer sun.

Where Sutton's features were heavy, Maddie's were light. He loved her eyes, would search them for the brown fleck just off center in her left eye, a pleasing imperfection in the blue green. Her forehead was smooth and her eyebrows arched brightly above her wide eyes. There was no flaw in her straight, small nose, slightly rounded at its tip. Her skin was smooth, and though browned by wind and weather, as soft as cotton.

Where Sutton had deep creases on his cheeks, Maddie bore small indentations, hints of dimples. Her cheeks were drawn and her small ears winged in front of her hair, pulled tightly back and parted in the middle. Her teeth, softer than Sutton's, were stained and the front ones in her lower jaw bent and crossed like pines in a forest. Aware, she smiled rarely and then only when a joyful or humorous moment caught her off guard. The corners of her small mouth turned downward, not in sadness but in caution above her small, square chin.

Together with her short frame and straight spine, her features suggested demur intelligence. When she wanted to affect a pout to feign disapproval, she could wrinkle her brow and pucker her thin lips in a way that was at once defiant and playful.

The girls rose from the bench and darted for the door.

She said, "No, no! Get the proper clothes on 'fore you go there. There's a hook of winter hangin'."

The younger one went to her bed for the handkerchief she always wore around her neck. The girls bundled up, and went outside, and Sutton sat for his alfalfa tea, and Maddie obliged. They said nothing, and soon Sutton left quietly.

She swept the dust and dirt into a pan and threw it out the door. She removed the dishes from the cupboard and again washed them. She wiped the churn again, wetted her cloth and cleaned the inside before returning its top, with its turn wheel and small gears. She folded the cloth and wedged it between the gears, then she pulled it through again and again to eliminate the dust.

When she finished her chores, she sat at the bench and prepared her pen, fountain and stationery. She could hear the girls outdoors, playing now. She smoothed the paper with her pen hand while holding it in place with her left. She would not complain of anything. She thought of her father's St. Louis home, and the tidiness of it. She pictured the heavy, Victorian divan and the ornate side tables, draped in lace her mother had crocheted. She wrote:

"Dear Father:

"*The girls have gone outside to do chores, and I take this opportunity to write. It is not yet spring on these plains, but it isn't bitter cold this morning either. If this nice weather holds, we will go to Rackett tomorrow to see Sis and Charles ...* "

Her hand lifted, and she leaned back, thinking of the floral wallpaper, the desk in the corner and its kerosene lamp aglow in her father's home. And then, without warning, she pictured Doc Bronson and his office in Rackett.

" *. . . We have been doing well. The days are warmer, and Will is preparing for spring work. We must make sure we have supplies before we are too loaded down. We are happy here. The fourth year is nearing. We are closer to Will's goal of owning our section. We have been healthy. . .* "

She put the pen down. It wasn't ill health but discomfort that took her to the doctor. Will was big and it was painful to receive him, but she knew it was her duty. She did not resent him, and neither did she enjoy him when he entered. She would keep her eyes open, and she would train her thoughts on the dirt and the dust, and she would plan her next defense against them. When he was finished. she folded herself into a tight ball on her side and whispered good night to him so he would know everything was all right. In the morning, after he and the children had gone outside, she would clean away the dried blood. She thought again of the doctor's examination room. She remembered sitting on a hard table made of oak and covered in linen, the walls papered with garish dark wallpaper, green with dull red flowers, gaudy and not comfortable like her father's home. A carbide light brightened the corner, resting on a small table. Behind glass doors in a cabinet, the doctor kept his tools. He had arranged bottles of medicines and tinctures neatly on the lower shelf.

He kept his desk in the examination room, and behind it were his books, some in English, some in German, some in French. A wooden box sat on one of the shelves and the doctor had gone there and paused while explaining to a puzzled Maddie that it contained the scalp of an Apache. He said it was the gift of his friend who was an Indian hunter. In the old days his friend roamed Texas territory killing Apaches and taking their scalp and right ear and redeeming them for fifty dollars each. The doctor held the box up and tilted its glass top so Maddie could see. He said he had other souvenirs, too.

She shuddered as she recalled the doctor's round face, his thin lips drawn horizontally, turned neither up nor down, expressionless. His eyes were so light blue as to be almost translucent, set uncertainly beneath his nearly absent eyebrows. His ears, barely visible behind his mass of sandy hair, clung tightly to his skull. His nose was lost between the penetrating eyes, so unremarkable and overshadowed that she could not recall its appearance. He seemed little taller than she because his strange personality seemed to diminish his stature.

All of this he betrayed with a condescending smile that seemed warm and comforting until combined with the fullness of the man's presence, the unlikely décor of his examination room and his inappropriate smile. She shook herself uncomfortably and renewed her train of thought.

". . . but there have been a rumor of measles. I hope the girls don't contract. They are healthy and active. Almy is such a reader. Do you have a book you could send her? She has read everything Charles and Sis have given her. She likes books about adventure . . ."

His library. Books on anatomy and poetry, complete works of Matthew Arnold and that new writer, Whitman -- that frightening New Englander Sis had mentioned whose thoughts raged beyond the bounds of decency. She had thought to ask for something for Almy to read, but she did not like his books. Then the doctor told her to sit on the cold examination table. He went to his shelves and immediately fingered the box. The scalp rested on a lining of blue satin, as if a corpse in a coffin. He held the box proudly and at the most unexpected moment approached her and quietly told her to remove her clothing so he could have a look, and she stepped behind the dressing screen. She trusted doctors, everyone did, and put on the gown after removing her clothes and reluctantly hung them on the hooks. Then she stepped from behind the screen to see him smiling beside the examination table, and she advanced haltingly.

". . . Viola loves her Pa and can't wait to work beside him. I think she's half boy, Father! Her energy abounds and honestly, I think she will one day run her own 'stead. She's a hand in the kitchen, too, and loves her chores, especially churning our butter, which she doesn't mind eating either. I must thank you for sending her the handkerchief Mother made before she died. Viola loves it and wears it

*constantly. The embroidered strawberries on it give her much happiness, I think . .
."*

Doc Bronson motioned her to the table, and when she was seated asked her how many children she had, and she reminded him there were Almy and Viola. He wanted to know their ages and she told him, and he said they must be pretty. She wondered how he could forget them, having seen them in Rackett. He asked her what her problem was, and she said she had felt pain at her time. I see, he had said. It is painful, she said, sometimes when my husband ... and the doctor said, I see. Then he said we shall have a look and placing his hand on her shoulder nudged her backward so suddenly that she lost her balance and hit the table hard. He smiled and put his hand under her at the small of her back and cupped it into a hard fist thrusting her hips up. Then, he withdrew his hand, and moved to each ankle, gripping them one at a time, and lifted them sharply to the table surface so that her feet were flat against it, and she held her knees tightly together.

" . . . Our winter supplies have lasted, but I long for something fresh. Will plans to make our garden plot larger near the pond where it is easy to get water. We shall have potatoes and cabbage again, and Will has become expert at making kraut. The bohemian family showed him; theirs is the best in this country. Turnips and parsnips, too, and onions and carrots. Vegetables keep well in our dugout and Will has made a door to make it easier to store them and handy to retrieve. Our neighbors are the best any prairie gal could hope for. We all have our own land and our own homes, humble but ours! There are no renters, Father, no renters here and we are free to do as we like. We will soon have our spring get-together. You should see this community of ours, growing and expanding. We have a nice spot by the pond where we can sit and eat and catch up. We have a close community, as fine as any there is in Missouri, Father . . ."

Doc Bronson took long to examine her, and he ignored her discomfort. He said nothing except hums and ahs and I see. She trembled when he touched her. He had pulled her gown down and she relaxed her grip on the table edge. He had gone to his cabinet of medicines and removed a bottle with a tapered neck and emptied its contents into a bucket by his desk. He said, you can wash this out and make sure you've got it clean. Then put on some petroleum jelly around its neck like this and you can help make yourself larger. Sutton is a large man, isn't he? Then he pushed her legs apart and said so faintly she could barely hear, "Like this..." and when the cold bottle went in, she shuddered and gripped the table and moaned. He smiled, but she saw something else in his eyes. She said she understood and hoped he would stop, but he kept on. She found his hand and pushed the bottle it held away. Then she said thank you. She quickly dressed and left the doctor's office. When she walked down the street in Rackett and past her brother-in-law's newspaper, she was stooped slightly and held her chin low and glanced upward only briefly when others passed. She wondered when she would do such a thing, maybe only in the outhouse or down by the lake alone. She told no one, but sometimes in her sleep she would cry out and Sutton would nudge her awake and say you've been dreaming.

"... I must close, Father, for we must make ready for our trip to Rackett. Lovingly, Your daughter, Madeline."

She folded the letter and placed it in an envelope she had made from a whole sheet of blank paper. She would post it in town.

3

Farmer

OUTSIDE, Sutton pulled the wagon into the yard, dug his boots into the sand as he moved backward, gripped the tongue tight in his hands. The back right wheel wasn't right, shuddered with each revolution. He dropped the tongue and went to the iron tire and rubbed his large hand across its smooth surface. He went for a hammer, and he rapped the iron with his hammer. He wanted a ring, but he heard only thuds, and dust puffed from between the iron tire and wooden rim.

He went to the sod barn and returned with two blocks of wood. He went again to the barn for the ramp and his wheel wrench. He rolled the wagon up the ramp and placed the wooden blocks under the axle to hold it. He removed the ramp, and the wagon hung with its right hind wheel suspended. He went to the hub, and with his hammer knocked the dirt and sand from the nuts.

He loosened them and then pulled the wheel. He rolled the wheel to the yard bench and worked the hub into the vise. He wrestled the large anvil, mounted on a stump, under the rim and rapped the tire all around to see the extent of the dishing. He had no wood to hot-set the loose tire, so he figured to use his sledge to pound it reasonably into shape. It would not hold, but it was the best he could do.

He examined the hub, and it seemed tight, but some of the felloes were loose. Then he returned to the wagon and examined the axle. It was bent. He crawled under the wagon and with the hammer rapped it several times. It did not yield and in aggravation he gave up. He went back to the wheel and its wooden rim and iron tire. With his left hand, he gripped the large wheel and with his right peened the tire above the dished areas. His large hand dwarfed the ash handle of the hammer, and his left hand almost went around the iron tire and rim. Two fingers, the pinky and the ring finger of his right hand lacked nails. He ignored the pain when the stubs bumped the wheel. He wore no ring. His wrists, thick from work, tapered from his bulged forearms but were nearly as wide as his hand. His nails underneath were caked in dirt and the surfaces jagged from coarse trimmings with his pocket knife.

He thought about the wear and tear this homestead had on his machinery, his animals, his determination and his wife. Maddie was more than a wife; she was his helpmate. She had often demonstrated her strength. She was methodical about tending to the everyday work that was their lives. They were stronger together than they could be alone. In the face of this ceaseless

challenge, their persistence affirmed that by fighting on they could endure. For Sutton, there was neither debate nor waffling between shall he or shall he not. He had long ago decided that doing battle against the Sand Hills was his choice and, and with Maddie's help, would be his reward.

He hammered again on the flattened areas of the iron tire, knowing his efforts would not be lasting, but might for a time secure the iron tire to the shrinking wooden wheel. As he worked, he thought better days would arrive. Perhaps there would eventually be a good return on crops and cattle. He knew that improvement in his circumstance would be incremental. At the end of the race, there would be reward; this land would be his. No man could take it from him, because he will have earned it with perseverance and determination.

Except Deast.

The intimidation was mostly bluster, but Sutton was not sure. Some had experienced his temper. His men were mean.

Viola admired her father, and in silence she watched him work. Maddie had pulled her long hair into pigtails and tied them with a small cloth bow, and each fell upon her narrow shoulders. She wore woolen overalls, a hole in each knee. As she nearly always did, she wore the white handkerchief with the embroidered strawberries around her neck. While Sutton worked on the wagon, she went to the water tank by the corral and got the chip wagon, its four small wheels rolling noisily as she pulled it toward Sutton.

As her father had done, she pulled the wagon onto a box so that the back wheel was suspended. She pretended to pull the

wheel, then turned the wagon to its side so she could hammer the tire, using Sutton's carpenter's hammer. Her rings echoed his, the din rising like a chorus of bells.

With no trace of a smile, he said, "This one's a tough one, eh Farmer?"

"Not for me, Pa! Mine's fixed!"

"It's no race," he said. "Do the work well and it won't need doing again."

He returned to his hammering and his thoughts. There had been definite improvements. He had the hut and the barn, a chicken house of wood, a pit toilet and a corral. He had strung more than a mile of fence, and there were no other enclosures.

Not so with Dimon. Deast fenced there before Dimon arrived, and the cattleman said hell would freeze over before he'd remove his enclosures. Dimon pushed back. Interior and the president himself were on the settler's side. If it ever arrived in this country, rule of law was in the settlers' favor.

The veins on his forearm swelled with renewing blood as Sutton worked on. Amid the rising din, the hub suddenly slipped from its mooring in the vise and the wheel tumbled to the grass. He dropped the hammer and lifted the wheel, placing it again in the vise. He tightened the jaws and set to work again.

When the iron had molded onto the rim, he loosened the vise and set the wheel to the ground. He went to the barn for grease and lubricated the hub thoroughly. He rolled the wheel to the jacked wagon and lifted the hub to the axle. He replaced the nuts and tightened them, pulling the wheel into place. He checked the true, then replaced the ramp and knocked the wood jack free,

and the wagon bounced onto the ramp, where Sutton quickly held it steady then eased it onto the ground. Tomorrow they would leave.

4

Almy

EVENING. Grace. Supper. Almy and Farmer washed the tinware and returned it to the shelf. Relaxed and quiet, Almy drew a deliberate breath and let it linger before she exhaled slowly. She loved her home. She loved that her father worked the earth. She loved living *in* the earth. She thought her home was the grandest house, as good as a church. She thought that when night comes, a home in the earth is warm and cozy. She felt safe.

She sat upright on the wooden bench and leaned her small back against the wall. Across the room she could easily make out the blocks of sod that her Pa and the neighbors cut and stacked to form the hut. She regarded how the blocks were stacked, interlaced like fingers for strength. She thought the textured wall interesting and as pretty as the wallpaper in her Aunt Mildred's house.

Above the cot where she and Farmer slept, she used a spoon to chisel a cubby hole for her books. Envious, Farmer wanted one, too, and together they dug a second private place and covered the openings with a piece of flour sack.

Farmer's treasures were collected from the pond and the grasslands, tiny mollusk shells, bits of antelope bone scraped from the sand, and wilting bunches of grasses. Before sleep, each sister would ensure each of their possessions was properly placed, silently repeating their mother's directive, "... a place for everything, and everything in its place." They arranged every item, as if all were part of a wealthy person's trove of priceless art.

Almy, now twelve, was nine years old when the hut was built, and she worked with excitement and awe alongside her Pa to help make this new, strange home in the ground. Now, as evening settled like cottonwood in a lilting spring breeze, she breathed in earthy air in a room draped in lantern yellow.

Instructed by their parents, she and Farmer collected cow chips, put them in the chip wagon, then placed them conveniently by the cellar door. Together they stoked the fire until the black-iron stove nearly glowed with warmth. Now she settled with her book, and re-read its pages. Farmer sprawled on their cot, and kicked her feet in the air as she spurred an imagined pony and talked with an imagined sidekick.

Almy tried to picture herself in a simple wooden home in town, like the girls in Little Women. Their home was delightful, she thought, but in truth she preferred her own place.

She thought: Of the sisters in the book, who am I most like? Jo? Beth? Amy? No, Farmer is like Jo. Maybe Meg: Yes, I ammost like Meg. Maybe one day I'll have another sister, and maybe another. And like the Little Women, we will play in our home and dream of full lives ahead.

She had an idea, and it was straight from the book.

"Let's play Pilgrim's Progress," she said to Farmer.

"What's that?" Farmer said.

"I'll show you. But first you have to know about the pilgrim, whose name is Christian!"

"I don't know what pulgrum is," Farmer said.

"Pilgrim, silly," she corrected.

"Oh, plilgrum. Mommy, when we get to Rackett, can I help Uncle Charles print?"

Maddie worked a needle through Farmer's white and red handkerchief. It was dirty with every sort of Sand Hills grime that Farmer discovered.

"My dear Viola, we will ask Uncle Charles. How on earth did you tear this?" she said.

"I was working with Pa," she said. "It got caught on the wagon."

"Where did you have your head to get your neck bandana torn? Never mind."

"Farmer," Almy said, "Pilgrims go on long journeys to find out about God. Christian has to carry many heavy burdens as he goes, as a way of being tested."

"I don't want to be a prilgam," she said. "I want to work with Pa and Uncle Charles."

Sutton pulled out his violin case from beneath his bunk and opened it as he had done thousands of times, before there was a sod hut and before they had settled in the Sand Hills. Since his boyhood in St. Louis.

The instrument lay like a preserved body in a wooden coffin, nestled in amaranthine velvet and wrapped in white cotton. He undraped it carefully, and removed it from the scuffed case. He lay the instrument in his lap and plucked the strings from bottom to top and grimaced at the disharmony. He went to the kitchen and returned with a cup, then probed his trouser pocket for his knife. He opened the blade and with it rapped the cup gently. "I believe that's a perfect A," he said with a smirk. When he had matched the string to the tone, he tuned the other three strings to it in fifths which he got by ear. He swished the resin across the bow. The stubbed pinkie and ring fingers dangled heavily, like a counterweight, as he drew the bow gracefully.

Almy persisted. She went to the box and put several chips into the burlap. She carried the burden to Farmer and commanded, "Stand up." When Farmer complied, she put the sack on Farmer's back and tied it there with twine.

"You're lashing cow chips to your dear sister's back, Almy? Let's use a more kindly burden, dear child. Use the ticking," Maddie said.

She returned the chips to the box and folded the burlap neatly before returning it to its place. With the twine, she tied the wadded ticking to Farmer's back, and the younger one's eyes widened at the excitement of a new game.

"You are no longer Farmer; I christen thee Christian, a noble pilgrim worthy of all cause and prefect to all challenge!" Almy said. As she announced her sister's new title, she lay her hand gently on Farmer's head, where her red curls piled like autumn leaves.

"I am Christian!" proclaimed Farmer.

"You must go forward, Pilgrim, and find your God! Do not dismay at the fortune, good or bad, that comes your way! Learn by your experiences! Draw closer to God and be His servant always!"

Farmer strutted diffidently across the dirt floor, unsure of just how a newly commissioned pilgrim should walk.

Almy reassured her with, "Behold the humble Christian who seeks to please god in all aspects of human endeavor!" Farmer paused by the stove, seized the broom, and turned it downside up, pretending it to be her scepter.

Maddie looked up from her darning, and said playfully, "Dear Christian, you have forgotten your mantle." She held out the repaired handkerchief and Farmer marched by with her chin now raised regally. She took the handkerchief, and with Maddie's help tied it snuggly around her tiny neck. The embroidered strawberries, bright red, complemented her hair and skin.

"If your grandmother could see you now, my sweet child! I do believe she would be very proud that her favorite hanky has found an important place on the neck of a humble Christian lady!" she said.

"Grandmother made my hanky?" Farmer asked.

"Of course! It was for her teatime with the fine ladies of St. Louis. But I think it is in its proper place now. You look lovely, sweet child," she said.

Farmer soon tired of the game and suggested her own. She took the bunched grasses from her cubby hole and waved them slowly as if stirred by the wind. She gazed intently at the grass and indulged her youthful imagination. She began to say a story.

"This grass grows in the special place," she said. "The Indians said the tall grass was the man and the short grass was the woman. They chased each other over the hills, but then came a strong wind and blew the tall grass hard. The short grass couldn't keep up and it fell to the sand. Then the tall grass felt bad and came back and said, 'Why did you fall?' And the tall grass bent over ... "

As she said this she turned her hand down so the grass made a pretend stoop, and she bowed politely with it. Then she continued, but no one was listening.

"... I will help you up, and we will go away to the hills and dig a place in the sand and we will have children. Just girls, and maybe one boy-grass. But then the wind came again and blew very hard this time and both grasses were blown all over the place... "

She threw her arms above her head and let the grasses fly, and Maddie looked up quickly at the sudden exclamation and chided her for being loud and messy. Farmer went to her hands and knees and whispered very quietly to the grasses as she picked them up from the dirt floor.

"Don't worry, Grasses. It will soon be OK."

Sutton scratched at the violin until satisfied with the tuning and began to play the pieces he knew by heart. The soddie soaked up the music and made the sounds soft and clear as if the music were being played in a velvet-draped concert hall.

"Play my favorite," Maddie said, and Sutton's thick fingers coaxed a vibrato from the old instrument. He knew the hymn from his childhood. The children continued with their imaginary games, and Maddie sang as Sutton played.

Popish reign of bloody terror
Passes around -- an awful night –
Now the cloudy day of error
Breaks away in evening light.

When the hymn ended, she looked at Sutton and he returned a welcoming smile. She thought of him in bed in their corner of the sod hut, where there was warmth and safety, and now her world was coupled uncomfortably with the doctor's strange directive. She thought she should feel safe, but oddly, she felt an anxiety inside as if she had suddenly stepped to the edge of a great cliff and peered down from a great height and felt she might fall.

The hut quieted, the children tired, and Maddie ordered them to bed. Sutton removed his trousers and shirt and crawled into the platform that was their bed. Maddie turned out the lantern and hesitated until the last flicker faded. Then she lay beside him and hoped he was asleep.

5

Widlund's editorial

EARLY ON Saturday, Charles Widlund opened the door to his newspaper office tucked conveniently between the bank and the medical office of Doc Bronson on Main Street in Rackett. The crisp breeze outside quickly gave way to the odor of musty newsprint, dried ink, molten lead, and charred wood.

He hung his coat on the clothes tree and removed his hat. He went to his desk, its roll top hopelessly disabled by the stack of deckled newspapers on the right-hand side, the back issues he kept handy when he was writing. The cubby holes overflowed with papers and envelopes. A spike, screwed into its leaden base, rested immortally at the left of the desk, dozens of slips of paper impaled on it. He leafed through the mess and found his spectacles on top of the desk, and he fitted them neatly behind his ears and adjusted the bridge on his straight nose. As he did so, he brushed and twisted the corners of his wooly mustache in a singular motion he had completed thousands of times. He wore black woolen pants, faintly striped with vertical gray lines, and fitted tightly to his leather shoes. Over his ruffled white shirt, he wore a woolen vest. The collar of his shirt was drawn with a black tie, hanging loosely bowed. His light brown hair was parted on the left at the deepest point of his receding hairline.

He sat in his chair and reached for the stack of notices. These must print in the next edition, on Thursday, and he would prepare them for his operator. He thumbed down until he came to the cutoff date for this edition, then took the stack with him to the Linotype. He placed them on the copy board with a note reading "4/4 legals."

The one on top caught his eye. It read:

NOTICE FOR PUBLICATION

Serial No. 014599 Department of the Interior,

U.S. Land Office at Rackett, Nebraska. March 12, 1907

NOTICE is hereby given that Meredith A. Tomppert of Rackett, Nebraska, who, on June 2, 1902, made Homestead Entry Serial No. 014544, for W 1/2 NE 1/4; NW 1/4 Section 3; E 1/2 NE 1/4 Section 4; T. 20, R. 43 W and the S 1/2 of Section 35 Township 21 North, Range 43 West of the 6th Principal Meridian has filed notice of intention to make final proof ..."

"I'll be damned," Charles muttered under his breath. He went to the stack of back issues and scanned for the issue last fall -- was it September or October? He checked the issues in September: two, nine, sixteen, twenty-three and thirty. Nothing. Then he found the Oct. 7 issue, and he turned to the back page where the legal ads usually were printed. As he had recalled, it read:

NOTICE FOR PUBLICATION

Regarding Serial No. 014599 Department if the Interior

U.S. Land Office at Rackett, Nebraska. Oct. 7, 1904

NOTICE is hereby given that above cited entry, filed over the name of Meredith A. Tomppert of Rackett, Nebraska, is challenged and entryman is advised to appear at this office on November ... "

The time from the challenge of the entry until the settler's intention to prove up seemed odd to him. How could that have been reversed so quickly? Maybe Sutton knew Tomppert, or maybe she was another of those widows in Omaha who had never set foot on a Sand Hills claim.

He continued with the organization of the next week's legal ads. The door opened.

"Mornin', Mr. Widlund."

"Mornin', Greek."

Seeing Pete Manitakis was a small relief. He was one of the young Linotype operators who enjoyed a wanderlust life with good pay, thanks to his command of the new machine that greatly increased speed in the newspaper business. He traipsed from town to town in search of work and adventure. He was uncommonly skilled, and Charles expected a short ride with Greek. He was handy at the Ludlow, could pull galleys and he had a keen eye for typos. Widlund knew he had the luxury of a little extra time in his week thanks to Greek. Operator skills were rare on the prairie, and so Widlund paid Pete a good wage. In return, Widlund had benefit of a more manageable week. For Pete, the arrangement meant he could keep his own schedule and be his own boss in all but name.

Charles rarely permitted himself to get too close to any operator, because their transience was legendary. Since he purchased the paper he had been often disappointed by no-show Linotypists. So, his trick was to issue paychecks on Monday. Pay an operator a week's wages on Friday afternoon, and the saloon and the whore house would have it all by Sunday. He applied any pressure he could to retain a skilled operator. Every two-bit town in the west had a newspaper, at least a weekly and sometimes a twice weekly or even a "daily," although most published five or six days a week, not seven. Charles's *Rackett Tribune*, itself a weekly, was packed with small liners and larger display ads which had become a showplace for the town's growing businesses. His paper was growing.

"Legals stacking up, Greek. If you find the opportunity ..."

"Boss, you're drivin' me to drink with your work ideals. Hell, there's plenty of time 'til Thursday. But, by god if you're frettin' and stewin' and makin' life generally unpleasant for your associates, I'll be the first to calm your frayin' nerves."

"Mighty obligin' of you, Mr. Manitakis, sir," was all Widlund could muster.

"Hell of a row at the Silver Dollar, Mr. Widlund, sir. Last night. I made some mental notes so's I could relay the information. Maybe make page one or somethin'," Greek said.

"Dammit, Greek, I'm not paying you for saloon rumors. Got enough going on with real people, so your bar friends and beddin' mates aren't among my principal interests. We're best to look after the pillars of this community..."

"The ones with money," Greek finished. "Hell, Mr. Widlund, sir, you're barely paying me for typesettin' far as I can tell. I hear the paper in North Platte is offering near twice what I'm earning here, but you understand, Mr. Widlund, I'm plenty happy workin' right here at one of the territory's finest newspapers and for one of the few men of high regard and reputation. Money's fine, sir, but just being counted among the giants in the newspaper world is pay enough, you understand. So, there you have it, and seein' as how I'm damn near a company man myself, I'm just tryin' to help out. And this here information I'm talkin' about didn't come from one of this here town's fine ladies (and Mr. Widlund, sir, I won't go on about this particular topic this morning, but this here town does have some fine ladies!)."

"For Pete's sake, Greek!"

"Yessir! For Pete's sake, and mine, too; I shall refrain from more reviews of this town's entertainment world. But this squabble -- I witnessed it personally, and I'm telling, Mr. Widlund, it's something you might want to know about. Some of this town's finest citizens saw it, too. Doc Bronson was in on it, the lawyer man, and the cattleman they call Deast."

Widlund's eyes lifted in a small but unnoticed betrayal of his interest. The Doc. Now what in the hell would the Doc be up to? The Doc, the sonofabitch Doc. He should tend to the sicknesses of his patients and keep his nose from the politics and policies of the folks trying to make the place better. If the Sand Hills were to settle at all, there needed to be a place for the entrymen as well as cattlemen. Money and power and downright ruthlessness of the cattlemen had been part of the game from the first; he knew that. Now the Kincaiders were helping to settle the place in, but some cattlemen wanted it all -- free land! Maybe they were right; maybe the land couldn't support a farmer and his crops, but no doubt the settlement itself was good for the region, good for business. Kincaid himself thought so, and the Congress agreed. Otherwise, there would have been no attempt made nor success achieved in expanding to a full section the land a farmer might claim to make a go of it.

Greek could see Widlund had wandered away in his own thoughts, so he dropped the topic and began his routine machine maintenance, then shuffled through the copy he was to set, organizing it for priority.

Widlund returned to his work. He thought about his brother- in-law. Sutton was mostly a stubborn man with hands twice as big as his head, but he toiled, and he and Maddie and the girls held on in hopes that a piece of earth would be their reward. Who could oppose the effort? Who would not lend them a hand or credit an account to help them achieve their humble dreams? If the elements and the land weren't enough, by God, they didn't need the devious impediments of greedy cattlemen like Deast.

Let it play out; let the policies shape to the realities, he thought. No man should have his way by ruthlessness. If a man with a newspaper had a calling, by God it should be to give a small voice to the underdog. No doubt about who was saddled with the underdog role here in the Hills. Simply by challenging the endless waves of sand, drifting, and held tenuously in place by vegetation at once mighty and vulnerable, these dreamers took on plenty. Waves and waves of sand, rolled by millennia of continuous wind, always, it seemed, from the northwest, so continuous that they formed an ocean of choppy hills that may as well have been a vast sea.

What's more, winter, cold, unpredictable weather patterns, and howling winds all added to the challenge. To that add summer, humid and hot, the wind blowing through the heat. Add to that the drought, the wolves, the blight -- a sea of enemies lined up to charge like battalions to front lines where some sorry man of dreams stands with his wife and his children, each waving their arms and bending their weakened backs against a sea of endless trouble.

And to that add the cattlemen and any conspirators they could bring to their fraudulent schemes to kick the entrymen out. Intimidation. Cruelty – anything to drive the homesteaders away. How many had gone back East, left their claim, simply disappeared, gone mad and been sent to an asylum? Mad with defeat, mad with wasted time, mad with weariness, mad with children claimed by fever, mad with dust and gritty sand.

"Greek, you got me now. What were you saying?"

"It was in the Silver Dollar last evening, sir, ... "

"I know it, Greek. You already told me that."

"... and Clem and I was talkin' about the settlement spreading. Doc and that cattleman Deast was talkin' at a table and then that lawyer man comes in. Sat down next to them and started talkin' low. Clem and I minding our own business until Lucy come over and of course we invite her to sit and have a drink .... "

"Lucy! For god sakes, Greek! She's sent half the county to the Doc. They're in cahoots, I swear. She infects 'em and the Doc gets his fee in coin or cattle to fix 'em. Ruthless rascals."

"You're right there, Mr. Widlund, sir, and thanks for that warnin'. But I'm a civilized man, sir, and any lady of the town who wants to sit and talk about the lovely life we lead out here on the plains of hell is welcome at my table, and I'm proud to be a man of sufficient means to buy the lady a taste of refreshment, providin' I hain't spent my fortune on literary pursuits."

"Very good, Greek. You're practically a pillar of this burg, and we need just a few more like you to bring us the brink of hell itself," Widlund said.

"Why thank you, Mr. Widlund, sir. Well then, sir, I hear that lawyer talk about some happenings out in the homesteads. Lawyer says some 'steader gonna be lying six feet under his tidy little hay field if he don't find a way to see his kin back East for an extended period of time."

"Oh, hell, Greek. That's nothing new with the Deast bunch. They'd use every bit of what little brain power they have to push every last settler off. Nothing new, unless you have an idea about how to stop 'em, Greek."

"I'm capable of operatin' your Linotype, Mr. Widlund. No other skill than that ... that and sittin' on a nag's back headed East."

Widlund returned to his desk, and shuffled papers. He tugged at his mustache and shuffled in his shirt. Doc in the bar with Deast and Jonas Buck -- Jesus! Widlund's position on fraud had been clear, but he wasn't careless; the reality of business on the plains kept him in check. He owned this newspaper outright, and his ideas and convictions would shape it. He had his own press, an office in a sturdy building on Main Street, and one of the first Linotypes in the area. He had a hard-working wife whom he regarded as the region's keenest intellect. Advertising and subscriptions were growing, he had a stockpile of newsprint and three barrels of ink, and had contracts for more of both. Receipts generally exceeded expenses, and the residual went into his accounts at the bank, where he held a seat on the board. Hope for the future was palpable in this town, and the law was beginning to check the wild men who would take matters into their own hands. The rail had punched through to Oshkosh and on to Rackett. The Sand Hills were alive with settlers, many newcomers to be sure, and some not as resolute as their predecessors who had first homesteaded forty years ago. The weaker ones couldn't make it, he knew, but others would.

What was most urgent was the full faith and power of the U.S. government. Until federal fencing and homesteading laws could be enforced, the bullying cattle interests would push folks around. They called the entrymen dreamers, and that was partly true. Many came with no awareness of what would be required of them just to survive. They were dreamers, yes, and Widlund counted himself among them. The bigger money was with the cattlemen, but the brighter future lay in the coexistence of both. There was no future for a place ruled by selfish men who either had it all or ruined the men they couldn't scare.

His mind racing, he went to his desk and with pen and paper began the next issue's editorial. He wrote:

"WE TURN back the clock this morning to remind ourselves and our readers of the burdens and opportunities this amazing land imposes. Not so many years ago, the great John Wesley Powell rode this land with his troop of explorers and mappers. The expanse was not lost on him, and we know from our own experience that the weather and elements visited upon him were no different than they are today: They arrive with a vengeance at times, and with a gentle, even alluring, beckoning at others.

"We refer to this excerpt from Mr. Powell's report to the U.S. Department of the Interior dated July 1861 (and for you occasional visitors to our offices here on Main Street who at this moment may snigger that your editor couldn't find his printing press, let alone a piece of paper, we rise in our own defense to say simply that we found these notes exactly where we suspected we'd left them, in pile number three to the right of your editor's chair).

"Mr. Powell wrote of our land:

" 'The grass is so scanty that the herdsman must have a large area for the support of his stock. In general, a quarter section of land is of no value to him; the pasturage it affords is entirely inadequate to the wants of a herd that the poorest man needs for his support. Four square miles may be considered as the minimum amount necessary for a pasturage farm . . .'

"The fine cattlemen of our county can attest to the accuracy of Mr. Powell's assessment; it takes no small amount of this land to support a row farmer, and the cattleman requires even more land for pasture. Add to that the occasional incidences of livestock lost to blizzards and to cruel deaths in drifted blowouts, and no knowledgeable man would deny a cattleman his need for vast and cheap grazing lands.

"But the unacceptable tactics of cattlemen who intimidate and threaten the newcomers proves another point: No region of this country can for any productive length of time endure without rule of law enforced by the representational governments we elect.

"Let the cattleman have the land he has gotten through fair play and hard work. To the other rascals who would defraud the government in its offer of free land to settlers, the penalty of transgression must be both swift and consistent. We hear with our own ears the rumors that fraud persists. We hear with our own ears the reports of fences strung illegally around vast tracts of land that belong to no one in particular, and to everyone in general. We hear even that intimidation and threat have not disappeared from our territory. These practices we condemn with *our pen and denounce with our voice. To the rascals we say loudly: You are desecrating the principles on which we can build a respectable and sustainable future.*

"We stand behind the federal lawmen who enter our county with intent to discourage and eventually end these abhorrent crimes. Let the settlers and let the cattlemen advance their operations, and to all we say: Do so with respect for each other and respect for the laws of our developing land. By no other means shall we advance our meager hold on this land and the harsh elements that it wields."

Widlund put down his pen and adjusted his spectacles. He picked up his paper and read through his editorial, composed, as it had been, without a single cross out. He intended to learn the Linotype operation himself, and once he learned to compose at the keyboard of the massive machine, he would use it as his pen. But for now, he was pleased to pen another editorial for the *Rackett Tribune*. His piece was fair, and it was right. He pushed his chair back and handed the copy to Greek at the Linotype.

"When you get to it, Greek," he said.

"Of course, Mr. Widlund, sir. Did you want to hear about the fight?"

"The what?"

"At the Silver Dollar. By god, Mr. Widlund; it was a helluva row."

"Greek, you didn't mention any fight. Now what are you talking about?"

As Greek launched into the story, the office door opened, and Widlund was drawn away to help a customer with an ad. The story would have to wait.

6

Loading up

BY MID-MORNING he was ready. He backed the mare alongside the tongue and lifted the harness to her broad back. He fitted the bit, then tightened the harness. The old horse bellowed full of air, so he kneed her. She relaxed into the leather, and he pulled it tight. He repeated the process with the gelding, more compliant. Sutton flipped the reins into the wagon and knotted them around the brake.

He went to the door and said, "We can load up now."

Farmer said, "The wagon is fixed, Ma."

"Take bedding and you can keep warm with it. Jensens won't have enough for us anyway. We'll have a lunch on the way."

As the family made ready, the sky brightened warm and still. To the west, gusts stirred invisibly above the landscape. Late as it was in March, this calm morning welcomed a host of waterfowl settling uncaringly on Sutton Pond. Missing though was the swish of wind in the little bluestem and lovegrass, almost as if the land were suddenly covered with fresh snow on one of those muffled winter mornings when nothing moves, and sounds lift and then fall without notice. Motionless the grasses stood like soldiers awaiting a command, orderly and neat. Such a pause was so uncommon on the prairie that creatures settled, too, as if a ceasefire had been declared by unseen generals.

The opportunity had not been lost on Sutton. With weather so ideal, the time could not have been better to make the journey to Rackett. Were this to hold, he could make the two-day journey, spend one night with Widlunds, and be under way for the two- day return trip. He hitched the team and loaded the wagon. Always cautious and intuitively prepared, he admonished the children to bring their bedding.

"Farmer! You can sit with me on the bench, but I'll carry the gun."

The rifle was usually with him, and the antelope and deer can beware, for one likely will be shot and dressed, then lashed to the wagon and carried to Charles's for laying up.

"Hurry, Farmer! We're going! No, you may not bring your little wagon. Almy! Bring your two favorite books, no more!"

He checked his repair and hoped it would hold. He went to the barn and put tools he might need into a dirty canvas bag. A hammer handle poked through a hole a rat had gnawed. He shuffled the contents to make room for a can of grease and dropped it in, too.

Maddie called from the dugout, asking the whereabouts of the water dipper. He didn't know and went to look for it by the pond. It was there, and he brought it to her, and she collected it with the water barrel which was strapped to the wagon. He returned to the barn and looked inside the bag to be sure he had everything. He carried the bag by its hemp handles to the wagon, found the leather straps at the wagon gate and lashed the bag there, out of the way.

Maddie hurried with a few last-minute items, and she tucked her small tablet and pencil into her apron pocket, where she had written the things she wanted to mention to her sister and to Charles. Almy arranged the bedding in the back, so she could read her book, and Maddie slipped beside her, and they cozied together. Farmer slipped onto the wagon bench and played with the reins, as if she would soon take control. Sutton walked thoughtfully around the wagon, his mental checklist working silently, and then placed his worn sole leather into the iron step and boarded.

There was no lock to fasten, no windows to secure, no doors to bar. To ensure her udder would be regularly evacuated, the milk cow was tethered to the wagon, secured there by Farmer's eager hand, as Sutton had directed. Chickens were secured in the coop and given extra grain. A coyote may take them; that was the risk, but no less risk, realistically, than any other day. A small store of root crops remained in the pantry, beets and carrots and blackened potatoes sprouting new white stems from dark eyes. Their belongings -- rudimentary furnishings, two tables and two platform cots, the kitchen tinware, shining proudly from places Maddie selected for them on the rough-hewn shelving -- all would neatly await their return. Maddie's obsession with cleanliness was obvious.

Sutton's improvements to his claim complied nicely with the government's requirements for Kincaid Act prove-up, but he could not possibly protect his spread when he was away. His entry, like the others in the region, was vulnerable to any jumper. If he didn't return, simple paperwork would follow, and the claim would be the jumper's, a bold grab of someone else's labor. Opportunists could pick up, and with half the work and a tenth the worry, hold the patent as their own. Report the abandonment, file a new claim, and the land was the jumper's -- unless the hapless entryman had meant to return, result of which was a mere prairie squabble and an occasional shallow grave for a crow-picked corpse. If the jumper were to survive, and the family murdered, it might take an extra effort and a cattleman's wealth to smooth things over, but the sale to that same cattleman would make the trouble worthwhile.

Things looked in order when Maddie said, "Who's that coming?"

A half mile from their place, where the rutted road to Rackett turned northward and wound up the windward side of the blowout, a horseman descended at a lope. Atop the thick workhorse, the horseman rode uneasily. In the still morning air, the sand rose and fell without dust. No sound could be heard. The horseman rode toward the house. When the face was discernible, Sutton shouted, "Dimon!" The man rode on until he reached the loaded wagon and said polite greetings to Maddie and the children.

"Sutton, there's news."

Sutton stepped down from the wagon and the two men walked toward the pond. Maddie and the two children returned to the dugout, leaving the two men to talk privately.

"It's Deast," Dimon said, "He and his men came upon me yesterday. I was retrievin' my sulky rake from the south bottom where the hay was good last fall. Deast and a dozen of his men. Henry Coulson and my son Roy was with me. We was tightening bolts on the rake. Rootes Jackson was helpin', too. The bunch of them rode up behind us, Sutton, their guns drawn."

Sutton said, "Sons a bitches. What'd you do?"

"No one spoke, so I said, 'Good morning and what does this mean?' Deast looks to me and says he's not ready to tell me just yet. Just wanna look at you, he said. One of the men was nervous on his pony and it stamped and then he spurred it and liked to knock me down, just to show hisself off. I said again, 'What is the meaning of this?' and Deast said to son Roy, he says, little boy don't you think you need to go over there and stand up toppa that ridge? I told Roy to stay put, but Deast said to one of his men, you take that boy up there and stay right there while I talk to his pappy. I said you keep your hands off'n that boy, but his man did as Deast told him, and Roy went along without a word.

"Then Deast said to me, 'You old sonofabitch, I talked to you like a man a few days ago about working this hay again and now you look to be ignoring me.' Deast was nervous and tremblin' with emotion. He said to me again, 'You old bastard,' and pointed his revolver straight to my head and said, 'Dimon, you are a liar and a thief. You old sonnabitch, telling me like you're gonna make a case in federal court about that fence yonder,' and he said to me, Sutton, he said to me, 'you make a case in federal court, and I'll put a fork right through to your heart.' "

Sutton pushed his hat up and wiped his rusty hair away to the side.

"Dimon, listen here," Sutton said. "The bastard's got no leg to stand on. His fence is on your entry; goddam it, it's illegal."

But Dimon went on. "Sutton, he and his men are puttin' the fear of God into us. They want us out, and I'm not so sure just how far they'll go. Said right there, if I would make a case in federal court, he'd kill me right on the spot or have somebody else do it, and he has his damn hired hands to do it if he ain't got it in him. After he said such to me, he rode direct to Henry Coulson and said, 'You old coot, I will kill you myself if you run any more lines or help any more of these goddam sodders survey out their claims.' "

Sutton said, "He'll run afoul if he messes with that man. Henry Coulson won't stand for it. He's surveyed out all of us and got here a damn site before the rest of us. He knows how to handle a rifle, too; everyone knows that about Henry Coulson."

"Well," Dimon said, "Coulson's friend Rootes Jackson weren't up to takin' his talk neither. Sutton, that black man's the bravest I've ever seen, and crazy, too. He stepped up right to Deast's horse and said, 'You ought to move on now, mister, and if you don't, you might want to get off your nag there and say something man to man.' "

Sutton said, "That Negro from down near Oshkosh? He's proved up, ain't he?"

"Yeah, he's proved up, and there ain't no takin' his land. But if there's any fight, I'll tell ya, I'd want him there after I saw him stand up to Deast.

Well anyway, Deast said to Jackson, 'You black sonnabitch. You just stand aside. I hain't got no argument with you unless you get to pushin' too hard. Then me and the boys here might want to help you think again about who you keepin' company with.' Why, Rootes Jackson started toward him, Sutton, but Coulson grabbed his arm and told him to stay. Oh, but then Deast turned and said to Coulson, 'I know you're a little deaf from firin' that gun of yours, but you'll hear this I reckon. You survey out any more of these claims and I'll put my rope around your wrinkled old neck and sling you tight against that fencepost, you old sonnabitch. And I'd horse whip you myself,' and he said going on, 'how'd you like that, Coulson? And Henry looked at him straight and said right back without blinkin' his eye, I reckon I wouldn't like that very much, Mr. Deast. I reckon that would make me right unhappy.'

"But that just seemed to make this beast of a man even madder, Sutton. He turned right around to his men and said, 'Now here we go for a little fun, fellas. You each go two to a man,' and they did as he said, and then Deast clicked back his revolver and the others did so just like him, and he leveled his pistol right at Coulson and then back to me, and he said you stay right where you be, and you watch what my men need to do right here to help you with your chores.'

"Now, Sutton, right then a man called Lonnie dismounted and came right to Coulson and me, and he picked up our pitchfork and said, you boys doing the wrong thing here, and you need to be learning some school lessons.' Then he ordered his men to unharness our horses and cut 'em loose, then they set to shreddin' the harnesses with their hatchets and knives.

"Sutton, I got no money to repair that damage. I'm done for. And that ain't all, soon as they done cuttin' up the harnesses, they started on the sulky rake and smashed it with hammers. Sulky rake I paid thirty-five dollars for Sutton! Harnesses ruined, too. How am I going to replace 'em? Deast musta seen it on my face, Sutton, 'cause he came over with a piece of the cut-up harness and held it in front of my face, sayin' 'Here's a little souvenir for you, remind you of your business in federal court.' "

Sutton paced away, his head down in thought and agitated. Then he squared to Dimon and said, "I'm heading to Rackett. The wagon is loaded, and the family's waiting. I need the time to think, anyway. Dimon, you go home. You and Coulson get your heads together and write down what happened. It's criminal, and it can't sit. Folks here have waited too many years for the law to come, and we still ain't got enough justice to go around with some of these crooks. I'll be back in four or five days. Then you and Coulson come over here so we can talk again. I'll be notifying what friends we 'steaders have in town. Now you go, Dimon."

The old man strode over to his workhorse and mounted. Maddie and the girls waved him goodbye, and he tipped his hat and said, "Mornin'" as he spurred the horse ahead. Maddie saw the look Sutton gave her and turned.

Sutton said, "We'll be goin' now. Step up Farmer." He pulled himself again onto the wagon and sat a moment.

"One more thing," he said.

He set the brake and Maddie said, "What is it?"

Sutton walked to the barn for the casings he had reloaded. One or two short of two dozen for the rifle, and a fistful for the revolver. They would not be as true as factory loads, but they'd bring down an antelope or scare away some other sort of trouble if needed.

7

The storm

THE RUTTED trail from the Sutton entry wound northeasterly toward Rackett through a depression between the rolling hills. No more than a half mile from the dugout, it bore leftward to climb the hill, which like all other of the sand hills, had drifted downwind of the prevailing northwesterly winds, merely one in an ocean of sand waves. Like a schooner on a tack, the wagon tipped as the sand pitched it leeward, but Sutton coaxed the team uphill and the wagon, half slipping, half rolling, followed.

The creak and groan of the old wagon filled the still air. Sutton slackened the reins and, looking to Farmer, motioned almost imperceptibly to ask if she wanted to handle the team. In fact, the team needed no reining; the horses would follow the ruts until stopped, a plodding, determined rhythm.

He instructed her to let the reins loose so the animals would not be distracted, then he hopped from the bench and half walked, half ran alongside the rotating rear wheel. The repair was holding, so he climbed aboard.

The sky above was deeply blue, the air warm. To the southwest, barely visible, clouds were building. It was a day before Easter, an inviting day, the end of March, winter bitterness surely behind them, and all of nature was beginning to stir in anticipation. With Farmer at his side, Sutton permitted his mind to forget the wheel and its imperfect turns. Farmer held the reins intently. Almy tried to read despite the wagon jerks and sways. Maddie reclined, admiring the sky and seizing the moment's peaceful respite.

"How far've we come?" she asked from the back of the wagon. "Not far; maybe a couple of miles."

"Why so quiet?" "Thinking."

"Dimon?"

"Yep."

"Tell me."

Sutton rode on in silence, and Maddie fell quiet to the lurch of the wagon. What was Deast up to? The man, by Dimon's account, was completely wrong. His fence was illegal. The government, if it ever showed up, would force its removal. Deast resorted -- and not the first time either -- to threats and intimidation. But this was outright harassment and property destruction. Dimon was scared, understandably. His sulky rake was destroyed, his harnesses shredded. He had no money, and credit would be hard to pry from hard-up merchants. Strapped neighbors would loan and give what they could, but most were in similar straits. Deast was well known in the county, given a wide berth because of his money and not liked. He lorded his stature over his hired hands, the stronger and more independent of them simply quiet and acquiescent because they needed the work, and the weaker a band of noisy yes-men. There was progress on the plains, but law was slow coming. By God, he thought, it must be brought, and if not by federal agents, then by resistance.

He thought of Charles. He seldom knew where his brother-in- law stood regarding these occasional range disputes. Business interests may have kept his emotions from boiling over; he seemed more suited to mediation than to confrontation. When there was an argument, it would usually be Charles who would fish for ways to bring reason to the discussion. Even in family squabbles he equivocated. He used his newspaper to advocate peace and good humor. Still, Charles had a strong sense of justice, and he always had supported Sutton's humble dedication to proving up. Sutton decided he would tell Dimon's story to his brother-in-law and at least have the benefit of Charles's counsel.

He would tell Maddie, of course, but not with Farmer and Almy around. He knew at times he wasn't careful enough with the children, attentive to what they needed to know, or from what they needed protection. Their life on the prairie was all they knew; to them it wasn't difficult or cruel. They were strong. Almy made herself knowledgeable, enjoying her books and indulging her curiosities and interests. Farmer, ever the helper, full of life, tough as whey, seemed as if she were born for this primitive way of life.

The horses stirred, lifting their broad noses to strain at their traces. They cocked their ears to a slight breeze and snorted loudly. Sutton noticed, vaguely, a change in the air. He asked Farmer for the reins, and sensing it was time, she complied. The wind picked up and gusted at times, unconvincing. The clouds which had been distant only minutes ago were now moving upon them, and the wind smelled oddly of rain. The blue sky darkened; the stillness that had characterized the peaceful March morning left in haste.

A crack came from the back of the wagon, and it limped with each revolution of the rear wheel. He stopped the team and went to the wheel. The spot he had repaired hadn't held. The wheel shrank beneath the tire, and the felloes near the loose iron tire moved with his hand when he tested them. One was broken. He looked carefully and weighed the options. Repair might work, but not here, and not with the weather building. They could go back, but Jensen's was no more than a couple of hours. He resumed his seat, lifted the reins, and pressed on in silence.

The wheel worsened, and the wagon limped with each turn of the tire. The horses seemed more nervous and lifted their noses to smell the air. Their ears tuned ahead and then back, as if pleading with Sutton to reconsider. Obediently they moved, but their attentive ears were turned to what was ahead, in the air, riding the wind. Sutton felt a storm, but he was determined. He slapped the reins across the animals' backs, loosening their bits and voicing a "Heah!" for their benefit and to affirm his command.

Farmer pulled her leg over the bench back and deserted to Maddie and her sister. Together they pulled in, snugging the ticking around them. They were silent, and when a sudden gust lifted the wagon slightly and then dropped it without warning, they each yelped helplessly. The wheel collapsed. The horses jerked the harnesses and traces. The swingletree behind them snapped to, and the chains clanked tight in unison.

"Whoa!" Sutton said.

He jumped from the bench and went to the wheel. His face dropped. He said nothing. They had come a mile or two, and he was sure the girls and Maddie could return to the soddie ahead of the storm. Then he could follow, leaving the wagon and leading the team. They would hurry to beat the storm. They must go now. He announced his decision.

"We can't go on," he said. "

"Why, Pa?" Farmer said.

"Repair didn't work, Farmer."

"I thought it did, Pa."

"It didn't. Storm's comin'. We're all going back."

He motioned Maddie out, and she looked at him with concern and disappointment.

"What should we take?"

"Just the bedding and what little else you can carry," he said. "You go now with the girls. I'll lash what I can on the horses and follow. Farmer, here; you take the cow. Lead her along and don't let go if she balks. Almy -- leave your books! I'll get them later. They'll be dry. Help carry the bedding. I'll be along as soon as I can get the horses unhitched."

They did as he said and started. He watched them go. Farmer raced ahead at first, too fast for the old cow, which bayed in protest, but then she and the cow found a pace and went along smoothly. Maddie and Almy, their arms wrapped around the bedding, followed. The cold wind snapped at their clothing, and they put their heads down and moved quickly away. Sutton boarded the wagon and goaded the team.

"Git! Heah! Heah!"

The wagon could not roll, so the horses dragged it. Sutton worked it away from the ruts and toward a blowout, where he thought he could better unhitch the horses and offload the contents. When the dragging wheel came out of the rut, the wagon lurched forward, and the axle caught in the sand. The team snapped to a standstill. Sutton brought the reins down hard on their croup. At his determined command, they reared, and that helped them dig their hooves into the sod, and their massive legs were taut. He repeated the command, and the animals pulled hard, and the wagon suddenly cleared. Team, wagon, and Sutton fell forward as if an opponent had let go in a game of tug of war. The wagon bounced into the depression, and Sutton stopped the team. He dismounted on the high side, and followed the traces to the breast collar of the mare's harness.

The weather had turned almost as if by a switch. The still day was gone. Now it was winter again, winds swirling counterclockwise as happens in a tornado. He looked in the direction Maddie and the girls had gone but could see nothing except dust- devil swirls, turning vicious. From the north, the air was bitterly cold, the temperature falling. The sand, sharp as brads and rocketed by gusts, ripped at his face. A gust caught his hat and it rolled away on its brim, like a wheel.

From the south, the moist wind became a gale and blew full on at the team. The horses turned their necks to glance the pelting sand, their ears cocked as they were helplessly held to their harnesses. The gelding, the more nervous of the two workhorses, reared and, Sutton was unable to hold the animal. The mare twisted its neck spastically, throwing Sutton away to the sand. He pushed himself up, and almost erect, he was thrown like a rag doll to the ground by another gust. He cursed at nothing and everything and pulled himself up again. This time, he threw himself to the gelding and gripped the cheek piece with both hands. The animal stomped in revolt, but Sutton held tight and the animal calmed. The mare, following, felt the reassurance, but still jigged nervously.

Sutton freed their harnesses and loosed the animals from the traces. His hands numbed against the iron and wood as he tugged at the fasteners on the swingletree. Rain now came in sheets and soon turned to piercing sleet, and then to snow, driven horizontally with the fierce wind. Sutton looked in front and behind, to his left and to his right, and he saw nothing beyond the wagon. The air was white with blizzard and dirty with debris. Snow, weeds, dust, fodder, and sand -- anything not held was moving before the raging wind. The atmosphere was electric, and lightening flashed at the dirty whiteness.

Sutton worked the horses free. Then he removed the bridles, one at a time, and the horses bolted away with the wind. He hoped to picket them but there was no opportunity. How much time had gone by? A half hour by now? Where were Maddie and the girls? Did they make it to the soddie?

Snow, drifting now as the winds rose to the lip of the blowout, began to accumulate in winnows as high as the wagon hubs. There was no other protection except for the wagon and the blowout. Sutton had little extra clothing, and Maddie and the girls had carried the bedding away. He searched for his wool coat and found it under the bench in the bed of the wagon. He looked for anything else that might help resist the cold. He found his leather gloves, holes in the finger ends.

He pushed against the leaning wagon and tried to tip it over. The wind pushed back, and he found that he could gain on it only by timing his efforts to take advantage of momentary lulls. Working it, the wagon began to rock. He yelled out to no one, a feverish yell, making no sense and only affirming his panic and desperation. The wagon suddenly lifted in a gust and his then fell, twisting his wrist. He swore loudly, and the oaths only drifted to nowhere as all else, to no ears, to no help. He determined to flip the wagon over and provide shelter. The heavy old cart groaned as it rocked, like a beast in mud. He tried using his shoulder against the sideboard, then shifted completely around and used his back. His boot heels dug into the snow and then suddenly slid from beneath him and he fell on his back. He lifted himself, tried again. He brushed the snow aside with his hands so his boots could find a hold in the sand beneath. He dug his heels deep, then pushed up with his broad shoulders, and the wagon gave way and came to rest on its right side. Now he placed his hands on the wagon bottom and shoved again, but the broad top of the wagon was dead into the wind. A gust caught the top side and skidded the wagon back into him, and it came to rest a yard from where it had lain. But now it tipped more into the blowout. With its new position, the wagon leaned, and before another blast could catch it, Sutton pushed hard, and the wagon turned upside down amid the drifting snow in the bottom of the blowout.

He lay in the snow, his heart racing. His head ached. He came to his knees and clawed the snow to crawl under the overturned wagon. Inside, he pushed snow aside to burrow into the space at the back where there was little wind. The cavern he had formed resisted the wind, and the air inside warmed from his own heat. He sat with his back against the wood of the box, his head bent forward for lack of space. He stretched his legs before him and breathed deeply. The wind lifted the wagon occasionally, sucked it upward then dropped it. It was dark beneath. White above. The bench kept the forward part of the wagon lifted, and Sutton could see the snow accumulating, covering the wagon slowly.

8

The others

FARMER thought she saw the hut.

She yelled, "There it is, Mommy! There it is! Look!" and she bounded ahead. Maddie thought she heard Farmer yell something that was lost to the wind. She hurried ahead but stumbled on a snag of bluestem. Almy, a step behind, helped her mother.

The wind lashed stronger than ever. Maddie and Almy searched the whiteout for Farmer but couldn't see her. Farmer raced toward the hut, but she lost sight of it. She fell into a depression, then gathered herself and ran again. Almy thought she saw her sister and yelled, Farmer! Stop! into the wind and white. Maddie and Almy groped along, snow drifting angrily. Their dresses stiffened with snow. Maddie until now had not worried, because she knew they all would be safe when they reached the hut. But Farmer ran ahead, on and on, as fast as she could maneuver in the drifts and whiteout. Her coveralls thickened with snow, and she stopped to brush them off. When she started again, she wasn't sure which way to go. She dropped the tether holding the cow and it moved away with the wind.

Maddie and Almy stayed together, helping each other, but they lost sight of Farmer. When the wind lightened for a moment, they thought they saw the hut and the barn, the cow moving toward it. They adjusted their course and had a bearing before the whiteout resumed. Then Maddie saw the soddie; it was more to her right. She yelled at Almy.

"Here!"

Almy found her mother. They went to the front of the hut and pulled at the door, but a growing drift had blocked it. The pulled together but it would not move. Then they remembered the back entrance, and when they went there, they found it exposed. Maddie pulled up and the heavy door rose, but a gust caught it and slammed it down again. Almy helped. This time they pulled the door open and went in. The wind blew in with them, and they reached to pull the door shut. It was heavy and would not move against the wind, so they both went outside and pawed at the snow to free the hinges. They went down the steps into the hut, holding the door as they went. A gust wanted to pull it up again, but they held tight, and it slammed shut.

They fell silent on the steps, breathing heavily. They began to shake with cold and exhaustion. They huddled in a quiet hug. Maddie stroked Almy's hair and began to weep. Almy looked up to her mother's eyes, and when their gaze met, she whispered Where is Farmer. It was more a statement than a question.

Together they went out again and into the blizzard. They yelled into the wind, Farmer! Farmer! There was no response. Their frozen clothing matted against them, but they pressed on. They returned to the hut, opened the door, and went in, and then gathered all the clothing they had and put it on. Then they went back out, and the blizzard had worsened. Maddie screamed shrills of urgency and panic. Together they moved about, yelling, and searching. They made their way to the barn, and saw the cow waiting by the stall door, her head turned away from the opening. They yelled inside the barn, but Farmer did not return their calls. They shut the cow in, then went back out the door of the barn, but it had begun to drift over, and they could not close it tightly.

They went to the outhouse and looked in there, just in case. Nothing. They went back up the hill, toward the abandoned wagon a long way off, and stumbled on drifts accumulating in the depressions.

The cold numbed them, but they would not give up. The drifts grew deeper, and the wind raged against them. The sky darkened with nightfall, but they still searched.

When there was no more light and their hands were numb, they went in. They lit the lantern. They built a fire with cow chips, and the sod hut warmed. Their hands tingled and regained color. They made tea but said nothing.

9

Survival

Sutton did not feel hungry, but he was thirsty. He ate snow, but it was laced with wind-whipped sand. Then he remembered the small water barrel strapped to the back of the wagon. The blizzard raged above him, but he decided to go out.

Darkness waited on the sidelines like an ally to the wind. Without light, he could not be sure of his senses. He pawed at the opening under the side of the wagon, and he made it large enough to squeeze through. The storm had only worsened, but he stood with his back to the wind and hoped for his family. He turned to his right first, because he believed that was the direction they would have headed. As he turned his head, the wind whistled at his left ear, and driven snow packed quickly in it. He yelled as loud as he could.

"Maddie! Farmer! Almy!"

Nothing, so he repeated in the other direction with the same result.

He stepped forward to yell again, hopeful, but he tripped and fell face down into the snow. With his back still to the wind, he stood again and yelled, and when he listened for an answer, there was nothing but storm. He turned back to the wagon and had to squint into the wind to keep the whipping snow from his eyes. He groped in the whiteness for the wagon and when he felt it, he moved along it forgetting about the water barrel.

He searched for the bench seat, found it, and then groped for the entrance. In the darkness he felt only the wood of the box. He pawed like a dog, flipping piles of snow between his legs. He dug left and right until he had widened an entrance, and he dove headfirst into it, pushing with his feet against the drift until he was under the protection of the wagon once more. He lay there motionless for a time, confused and tired. He wanted to sleep. He snapped upright and yelled No!

He rubbed his hands and slapped his cheeks. He brushed the caked snow from his eyebrows and hair and away from the inside of his collar. He fished in the drifted snow for anything remaining from the wagon load of supplies they had packed.

He stilled himself for many minutes to rest and to reason. He wanted the water, decided he had best go for it. He stuck his head through the entrance and into the wind, then pulled himself out with his arms in the snow. On his knees and hands, he followed the edge of the wagon until he came to the back of it, then worked slowly to find the water barrel. The tool bag was there, but the barrel must have fallen when the wagon overturned. He made wide sweeps with this hands and arms, hoping to locate it. When he had searched the area at the rear of the wagon, he moved to the windward side. Deeper in the blowout the snow had drifted above the wagon.

He found nothing. The wind howled above him, and the blowing snow soon drifted over his legs. He could not move, did not want to move. He knew he must. His mind. It must remain in control; his body wanted only sleep. He pushed himself forward and on to his hands and knees and crawled downwind. His hands went easily into the snow where it had not yet crusted, and he felt the barrel. He dug until he was able to push his hand beneath it and pull it to his chest. Then he crawled quickly toward the entrance he had made, but it had partly drifted over, and he had to dig it open again. He pushed the barrel inside, stuck his head through, and pushed himself again inside and lay prone, the small barrel under his heaving stomach. Then he rolled off the barrel and searched for the bung, and when he opened it, the water inside was frozen.

He untied his shoelaces and removed his frozen boots. He pounded at his feet with his fists. He put the socks inside his coat and under his arms. When the socks felt warmer, he put them on, then he sat on the boots to warm them.

He kicked his feet into the air, lying on his back and yelling loudly with each kick. He turned onto his knees and kicked his legs backward. He leaned his back against the snow and gave up his flailing. He rubbed his hands quickly, but he felt nothing at the ends of his fingers.

10

At the hut

ALMY INSISTED, screaming in panic. Maddie pulled on her warmest clothing, and as she did, Almy clung to her. When Maddie pushed her away so she could open the cellar door, Almy became hysterical, sobbing and screaming.

"NO! NO! Mama! NO!"

Maddie was herself in tears.

"Almy! Stop! Calm yourself! You are to stay here. Keep the fire low and keep it warm for when I come back with Viola. Do it! Get busy!" Almy would not let go. Maddie tried to reason with her, but in frustration and urgency, she shoved her daughter to the floor of the hut, then pushed the door open and went out. The wind grabbed her garments and whipped at her harshly. She held the door against the wind, then yelled below, "Stay here!" She let the door slam shut and could not hear Almy's frightened wails. She faced the wind, and its howl rose in her ears. As she turned away, she felt the snow hit at her cheeks. She went to the front of the hut where the drifts were deepest. She could not see the top of the door. She turned and trudged through the drifts on the southeast side of the hut toward the barn, and when she got close enough to see its vague shape, she looked over her shoulder to the house, but she could not see it through the whiteout. She went to the barn entrance, but the drifts had nearly covered it. So, she went up the drift, pawed with her hands until she could enter a small space at the top. She went to the workbench and found the rope. The coils were heavy and frozen. She pushed her head and left shoulder through the coils and held the rope to her chest. She went out the way she came in, then, leaning far into the wind, she groped through the whiteness toward the hut. She hoped only that she could find it.

She found the handle to the cellar door and tied one end of the rope around it. Then she let it pay out as she moved away from the hut. Her instinct was to go into the wind because it was in that direction that she last saw Farmer. She made very slow progress. She fell often, and once dropped the coils of rope in the snow when she put her arms down to catch herself. When she recovered the rope and placed her arm through the coils, it was covered with snow and her hands felt the cold through her woolen mittens. Her falls frustrated her more. She tried to collect her thoughts and make her best judgments, but she was frantic. She hoped Sutton had found Farmer. That was the story she repeated. He was very strong. He kept them safe. But he was not here. She pressed into the wind and when she came to the end of the rope, she retraced her steps. She thought to move laterally. The rope if tight would guide her in an arc. She didn't know which way to turn, so she arbitrarily went to her right. The end of the rope fell again, so she stopped and tied it around her waist, then pulled herself further away until it was taut again. She continued to move to her right at the end of the rope. She stumbled into a small blowout, buried to her waist in the drift. She found her footing, and then pulled closer to the hut to slacken the rope and again moved to her right. She had gone a short way, and neither she nor the sweeping rope found anything. She screamed suddenly in frustration, "Viola!" and the wind muffled her scream in its roar and carried her call away. She went the other way, returned to her original point, and moved beyond it to her left for about the same distance. Again, neither she nor the rope found anything. Then she went another distance further left, in the same manner. Nothing. Then she returned to the far right and went out more and more and still found nothing. She decided to shorten the distance, thinking she would find something in the areas that the rope had skimmed over. She came back toward the hut where she thought the snow was deepest and began to move in that area. The drifts were much deeper here, and she reckoned she had moved into a depression. She tried to recall how the terrain had been before the snow, but she had never noticed the roll of the hill above the sod hut. Now she knew there was a place where the ground dipped deeply.

She sank to her chest in snow. She stroked like a swimmer, and she pushed her stiff legs in front of her. She flailed her arms above and beside her and made a hint of a pathway. She looked behind her and noticed the rope had caught on something and was bent at that point. She tried to lift the rope over the object, but it caught on something, like the leafless branch of a tree. But she knew there were no trees. She turned and moved toward the snag, pulling on the rope as she made way, but it would not come free. She reached the place where the rope had caught and flipped at the stiff rope to get it free. When it did not budge, she went closer still and grabbed the rope at the very point where it was caught. Her hand had come against something rigid. She could not see it clearly. She brought her other hand to the same place and cupped them both around the object and felt it up and down. She could see the rope was wedged between a pointed finger and a curled thumb on a little hand reaching above the snow. In the next few moments, Maddie etched everything in her memory, and it would never fade. Farmer's arm was stretched upward, straight as an arrow up, and the tiny forefinger on which the rope was caught was itself pointing up but curled gently, like Adam in the painting on the ceiling of the chapel.

The other fingers curled gently beside the first finger, and the little thumb, with dirt beneath its nail, was rigid. The sleeve that had been around the small arm had fallen below the wrist. The arm was nearly normal in color. Maddie did not scream in horror. She did not cry out for Sutton, for Farmer, or for Almy. She did not protest to God, nor did she curse. She was buried nearly to her shoulders in the drifted snow. The icy wind rushed around her bonnet, and her cheeks were raw and purple with cold. Her own worn hands cupped in them the stiff hand of her youngest child. She cocked her head slightly to her left and brought her chin low, and in this position, she looked like the mother of God in many paintings in many chapels in many places. She brought her eyes upward and beheld the frozen hand and caressed it as if she were putting the child to sleep. She leaned forward, bending only at her neck and shoulder, and pressed her own cold lips against the frozen forefinger. She kissed the small hand, and did not move for many minutes, waiting for something that never happened.

She let go and turned slowly toward the hut. It was easier to move in the direction she had come, because the snow there already had been moved and trampled and it parted with little resistance at her retreat. Despite the drifting and the howling, she found her way. She gripped the rope and ran her hands along it as she moved to her dugout. Once at the door, she untied the rope from her waist, and removed the knot from around the handle. Then she stooped and with her back and knees lifted the heavy door and as she did the snow fell to the hinges. Inside Almy screamed, "Mother!" so loudly that Maddie startled and then she continued her slow descent into the dugout. Almy ran to her and hugged her tightly, but Maddie gently pushed her away and turned to close the door. Where is she, Mother? Where is Farmer? Mother! Isn't she there? Couldn't you find her?" Maddie said nothing. She removed her outer clothing and placed the garments on the pegs. She put her cold hands to her cheeks and rubbed the blood into them. She went to the stove and lifted the cover and stoked the chips to revive the fire. She said, "Would you have some tea with me, child?" Almy put her hands to her gaping mouth and stared at her mother in shock. Maddie turned from her, and smiled gently as she returned to the stove and lifted the kettle. She went to the basin and poured the airy contents of the dipper into the kettle opening. She began to hum peacefully. But there was no water in the basin, and none came up with the dipper. When she placed the dry kettle back on the stove it made a hollow sound, empty with nothing to offer. The black stove was warm with its small fire, and the kettle rested hopefully there. Maddie turned and went to the table and sat quietly. She soon rose and went to the shelf for her cup. Then she went to the kettle, lifted it to pour, and then placed it habitually back on the top of the stove. She carried the empty vessel to the table, placed it there and sat. She gently lifted her arms and let down her long hair, and stroked it repeatedly in long, graceful movements, working slowly from the top, and when her cold fingers came to the end of the strands, she twisted the hair slowly and then let it drop so she could repeat the motion. She hummed, and Almy listened closely without speaking. The words from her mother's mouth were the same hymn that Sutton had sung in the upturned wagon.

Now the cloudy day of error/Breaks away in evening light.

Almy sat watched without speaking. Her mother looked in her direction but didn't say a word. Almy rose, went around the table, and stood behind her mother. She placed her hands on her mother's shoulders and leaned to kiss the top of her mother's head. Maddie seemed to relax to her daughter's touch, then suddenly rose. She turned abruptly to Almy, and the expression was something Almy had never seen, her mother's features distorted and grotesque. She wanted to scream, but she did not. Maddie looked not at her, but through her. There were no words.

Maddie jerked away, went to the pegs, and put on her coat and bonnet in hurried movements. She went to the corner by the stove and picked up the old broom then rushed to the door and pushed it open. She went up the steps and into the cold. Almy ran after her, but the blowing snow and cold checked her. From the top step she peered deeply into the whiteness and could see her mother rushing up the hill, falling into the drift, rising with the broom over her head.

She yelled, "Mother! Mother!" but Maddie did not acknowledge her. She kept on toward the depression where her Viola stood frozen. Almy could see only Maddie's vague shape in the whiteout. The broom rose and fell on something there in the snow, which Almy could not see. Again and again, her mother lifted the broom and brought it down fanatically on the little hand. She pounded at it that way as Almy only watched, and when the wind died intermittently, Almy could hear her mother say, over and over, "Stay down! Stay down!"

11

The discovery

SUTTON LiSTENED and heard no wind. His snow cave had warmed. He was comfortable, and there was no longer any pain in his fingers. He stuck his head through the opening and saw the landscape leveled with drifts in low areas and blown-dry ridges elsewhere. The sky was blue, and the sun bright. He shielded his eyes from the glare. As much as anything, he wished he had his hat.

He pulled himself from the upturned wagon and stood. His bones ached with stiffness, but he was generally warm. A hunger grew in his belly, and he was again aware of his thirst. He moved around the wagon and climbed to the highest point of the hill. It was windswept, and the tufts of grass stood as sentinels, hopeful and eager.

He looked to the southeast, in the direction of the hut, but it was not visible to him. He rubbed his hands together, and when he felt nothing he lifted them to eye level and held both hands palm side in. The color was not right. He turned them and examined the backs. The fingers of his left hand were swollen and red near the knuckles. He looked at the fingernails and they were purple and then black at the tips. The index and middle fingers were the worst. The left thumb was red at the tip. His right hand was blacker at the tips of the fingers. The nails, worn and ragged, were white at the edges and contrasted grotesquely with the deep purple, almost black, cuticles. The smaller fingers that had been amputated in the rake accident were nearly normal. He started toward the hut and his head filled with anxiety. He was reasonably sure that Maddie, Almy and Farmer had made it to the hut, but he worried about the livestock. He feared the worst for the horses. He was sure Farmer, speedy and determined, would have put the cow in the barn, closed the stall barricade and spread hay for the beast.

He carefully examined the crusted snow and chose the path least likely to cover a blowout. He was often wrong. When the crust gave way and his leg went through, he would be buried to his waist. Extracting the buried leg meant pushing with the free one, and often the process simply repeated itself until he managed to attain the lip of the blowout where the snow wasn't as deep. He foundered in another deceptive drift and was in snow to his chest. He used his arms to pull and his legs to push and he eventually freed himself.

He traversed two small valleys and on the third ridge he could see his sod hut in the valley below. From the chimney, there were

vapors that wrinkled the cold air, but no smoke. His pace hurried, and he often fell.

When he came close to the hut, he noticed vague tracks. It was not clear to him why there would have been need to come and go, but he dismissed the situation, affirming at least that the family had made it to the soddie as he expected. He went on to the barn to see if the livestock were there. The opening was drifted over, so he abandoned the idea and went to the cellar door. He opened and went in. There was no greeting.

He hollered, "Maddie? Almy? Farmer?"

No answer. He felt the stove, and it was warm. Two cups sat on the table, both empty, and neither had residue in the bottom. The water pitcher was nearly full. He looked to the coat pegs, and they were bare. The beds were cold. Neither pots nor pans had been touched. Tinware remained neatly arranged on the shelf.

He sat in the chair and hung his head in thought. He looked at his fingers and wondered if any would survive. He went for a cloth and put it in a pan and added water from the pitcher. He set the pan on the stove then opened the fire box door and added chips. He returned to the chair and waited. When he thought it had been long enough, he took the moist cloth from the pan and held it to his cheek. It was warm, so he wrapped his right hand with it. He went for a second cloth and repeated the procedure for his left hand. With both hands warming, he walked about the hut, trying to piece together what had happened.

They had been here, but why had they gone? And where?

He brought the cloth on the right hand to his cheek and it felt as cool as the room, so he removed it and placed it in the water

to warm again. He did the same with the wrapping on the left hand. He did this for several minutes. Then he wrapped each hand in dry cloths Maddie used for a towel. The wrappings were clumsy and loose. He went to the door and went out. He saw the tracks up the hill, and wondered what would have taken them there. Then he saw the tracks down the hill, toward the road and in the direction of the Adams place, their nearest neighbor to the east. That made sense; they would have gone for help.

The tracks were not drifted over, and he followed them. He guessed that when the sun rose and sky cleared, Maddie and the girls had gone for help. He hurried.

When he came to the top of the hill, he saw a small wagon pulled by a single black horse. Ahead of the wagon was one man, leading the animal and the wagon. Behind were three more men. In procession, they marched in single file, and the shapes of the men and the wagon and the horse were black against the glistening snow. They moved slowly, and their heads were down. In the still, cold air, he could hear the muffled clop of the horse and the creaks of the old wagon. They were moving along the vague road to his entry. He could hear no conversation among them.

He paused and took it all in. He raised his head to the sun, now midway across the southern sky where not a single cloud contrasted with the deep blue. The sun was bright in his eyes, and his nose tickled and he sneezed loudly. He widened his stance and rose his arms in unison and flapped them like a bird as he yelled in the direction of the procession.

"Heah! Heah! Hello!"

The men, the wagon and the horse continued with no mind. He yelled again with more desperation and this time the lead man pulled up the horse, and the wagon fell silent as it came to a halt. The men following stopped, lifted their heads and saw Sutton on the top of the hill, waving his arms and jumping. They seemed surprised to see him, and in a dumbfounded manner stared quietly with no response. Then the first man dropped the leader rope and after a moment he recognized Sutton, as if he expected it to be someone else.

The man picked up the leader rope and the procession began again without a word. Sutton went toward the men. When they met, he could see his neighbor Jay Adams in the lead. At the rear were his boys, who were named Wilbur and Jesse. The third man was his neighbor William Lukasiewicz.

Sutton greeted them quietly, and Adams said, "Sutton, Bill's going to take you on to our place. Maddie is there. We've come for some things and will return."

Sutton said, "What things?"

Adams lifted his bowed head and his eyes met Sutton's. He said, "It's not good."

Sutton searched his neighbor's eyes for meaning. The others remained a distance away.

Sutton said, "Is Maddie all right?" Adams said, "Yes. She's OK, Sutton."

"What about the girls, Jay?" He grabbed Adams' shoulders with his wrapped hands and shook the man as he asked again loudly, "What about the girls?"

Adams looked away and said almost inaudibly, "We've lost the

little one, Sutton. We've lost little Viola. We've come to get her." Sutton could not understand. He said, "NO! I'll come with you!

We'll find her!"

Adams said, "No, Sutton. We will get her. You must go to Maddie. She needs you now, and we will get Viola."

"You know where she is? She's OK?" "We know where. Maddie needs you."

Sutton whirled. He started toward his home, then returned to Adams. "Where?"

Adams took his wrist in his hand and looked deeply into Sutton's eyes. He said as softly, as tenderly, as he knew how, "You go with Bill and be with your Maddie and Almy."

12

The stories in town

THE STORM had lasted three nights, and on the afternoon of the fourth day, the clouds lifted, and the thermometer dropped. The clearing skies brought colder temperatures. In Rackett, people bundled up and began to move around town. There was talk of nothing but the storm, and people already had begun to call it The Great Spring Blizzard of 1907.

There was much concern about lost cattle. Some said the livestock would turn tail to the wind and wander as a herd downwind until they foundered in a blowout. It was that simple. They were stupid, like sheep, and would go into the blowout, sink, and then be unable to get their feet under them enough to push their way out. There they would slowly freeze, the nerveless hooves first, and then the cold would move up and into the hindquarters and shoulders, and when the heart and the other organs would shut down, all that later would be discovered would be the carcasses frozen just as they were when the heart stopped.

Old timers recalled the blizzards that had come before. That one in '73 killed the schoolchildren, but it was in winter. No -- yer thinking '88. Seventy-three was in spring! Hell, that was clear into April. And it came on like this one here so fast that the children were trapped on their way home from school. Yep, that's it. There was that teacher over by Ord, and some called her a hero 'cause she was smart enough to tie a rope between her schoolmarm house and the classroom where the children were trapped. They all made it, 'cause she could move them to her house and there was fuel enough to warm 'em all. Food and water, too. Just plain lucky, everyone said. The papers tried to make her into a hero, and they was right to, by gawd, but she just said that was all hogwash 'cause anybody would do the same. One heard of another awful storm, maybe that same one ya'r talking about, 'cause I don't remember the year, but I'll tell ya they found one ol' boy frozen right between his two horses -- the three of them there in a blowout frozen solid, like a statue in a park.

The door to the newspaper office was drifted over and Charles Widlund had to borrow a shovel from the bank next door to dig it out. When he put in the key, it must have been moist, because it froze inside the old lock. He found he could turn it back and forth until it finally worked free and clicked, and he went in. The paper was days late already, but people would want to know what he found. He took his pad and went to the grocer, and before long he had filled several pages with notes.

There were many stories. Up at the Davasher entry, just a short way from town, there had been an awful drift that buried the house and the windmill. They pushed a pipe up through the drift to have breathing air in their soddie. The windmill was in the low draw and was buried. That drift was said to be thirty feet deep.

In town, the old banker, Evan Gates, had watched the temperature. He said it was fifty-five when the storm moved in at about noon that first day, but by midnight it was 20 below.

There was a man gone missing over near Oshkosh, rumor had it. He went out to the neighbors, and it was a fine day, but before he even got there he wandered ahead of the wind and was lost. Maybe they'd find him. Yes, maybe so, someone said -- next July. Widlund did his job, gathered the stories, and made his way to the office to start making sense of them. Pete finally came in and warmed the Linotype, which had gone cold after three days. Widlund sat at his desk and wrote and when his paper was filled, he took it to Pete who set it.

He thought with disdain that people seemed to wear their storm stories like badges of honor, as if the most atrocious of them deserved special recognition. He disdained his own work at that moment, realizing that he selected the worst hardships and wrote about them first. People wanted to know just how bad it was. He wondered about Sutton, but he wasn't worried. He knew his brother-in-law and figured he was too stubborn to let a storm take him down. He knew precautions would have been taken, the chip box filled, the family snugged.

He and Mildred, meanwhile, had spent the nights in their two- story home at the edge of town. The cold and the blowing snow had come right around the window frames and collected on the sills in tiny drifts. The windows had iced over, and Mildred rolled towels and snugged them against the casings. She got out extra blankets and spread them on their bed. They slept snuggly, but these had been the coldest nights he'd ever known. He and Mildred in their wooden home had been cold but safe, but he knew it was no warmer, probably colder, in their frame house than the soddie would be, dug into the hill and protected from the wind. Even vegetables kept there through the winter. The Suttons would be fine.

Pete had little to say, and there was plenty to do. They could run the press tonight and have something out tomorrow. They'd print extra copies, knowing the freshest edition would be in high demand. Later they could follow up with more stories and better detail. In a corner of his mind, Widlund knew this storm would be a windfall for him. This part of it he enjoyed. His blood flowed with excitement, and he could call on his best skills to gather and report the news. There is a benefit to him, and he suspected to others, when an uncommon, calamitous event comes along:

Of necessity people spend more money, at least if they have it to spend. The uncommon storm provided a break from the routine as well. The squabbles and political tiffs for the moment seemed small and were put aside, as one might set a glass of brandy on the parlor table, then pick it up later with particular interest and renewed delectability. With the storm, the focus had returned the community to a more basic level of existence. People united in a struggle important to all of them. The normal jockeying for advantage was for the moment forgotten.

Pete interrupted.

"Say, Mr. Widlund. Take your mind off this horrible turn of nature for a moment and let me tell you more about that conflagration at the Silver Dollar. Do you recall the news I had hoped to impart to you before this calamity got in the way? I'd like to finish my story, if now is a good time for you, sir."

"Sure, Pete. Why not? People having a hell of a time just surviving this storm, but you've got more important matters concerning the administration of this town's underbelly. Might as well bring us back to earth."

"Might be I can bring you below God's good Earth, Mr. Widlund, sir. You know as well as I that these terrible events here in this glorious Eden you call Rackett, Nebraska, are coordinated with glee and for purposes of entertainment by the angels up above, and some of them not there at all but fallen to dark places at the center of hell, I might add."

"Yes, Pete; I had forgotten your command of Holy Scripture."

"Well, sir, that's right nice of you to remember the heritage of the Jews and, furthermore, God's gracious expansion into the territory of the gentiles, but let's not omit, sir, the consequential contributions of the great Greeks themselves. "

"Least of them you, my dear professor."

"Yessir, well now. Ahem. As I was about to say, sir, I'm prepared to suggest that the events at the Silver Dollar and those rumors circulating in the mills of this here town's elite are not entirely unrelated."

"Pete, your intelligence is without parallel. Talk sense or you'll have that Linotype speaking Greek, too."

"What I mean to say, sir, is there is a certain settler who isn't high on the social list as this country's foremost cattlemen. And that settler isn't much known to you or any others here, because his skin is as black as your inkpot."

"A black man. Is his name Jackson? I've heard of a black settler near Oshkosh. And how, Professor, does he relate to your narration?"

"I cannot say his name, sir. I do concur, however, that he is a proved-up entryman, and has his rights under the law just as any man. His homestead is in the township south of here, and I've seen him twice in my life. Once was in Oshkosh, and the other was the night to which I now refer. The night at the Silver Dollar."

"Yes, the saloon. Go on, Greek."

"Doc Bronson was there," he said.

"Yes, I believe you mentioned that before."

"And the county attorney, whose name I believe is Buck."

"Yes, County Attorney Jonas Buck."

"And the cattleman, Deast."

"As fine as we have, and as likely to be where you have placed them as the ladies of the quilting society."

"On that point, sir, you will have to rely on my veracity."

"All right. Of course. Carry on, professor."

"I cannot report what was said, except that the Moor in this play, the man you call Jackson, rose to his feet and said to the honorable cattleman that he'd regret it if he ever set foot on the Dimon land again."

"For Pete's sake, Greek. He must be talking about Dimon, south."

"I think that's correct Mr. Widlund. And Deast came at that man with a knife. And this is what he said, sir. I report it with utmost confidence." Greek paused to collect his thoughts. He took a breath, puffed his chest out, raised his chin and spoke as if a stage actor.

"He said, 'I'll take you down, you miserable black sonofabitch.' He came at Mr. Jackson with a snarl that could scare a wolf. But the black man – oh, this man Jackson is a giant, as strong as he is courageous. -- he seized Deast's hand at the wrist and squeezed it hard, and Deast flailed at him but to no good, and Jackson just squeezed with no expression on his face until the knife drooped in Deast's hand and then dropped to the floor. Then he twisted that man like a pretzel and brought his knife hand up behind his back and lifted it high to his neck and, I swear, Mr. Widlund, the twisted arm snapped and popped like water on hot grease. You could hear it straining at the ligaments!"

Again, Greek paused and stole a glance at Widlund to see if his drama was having the effect he wanted. Widlund was attentive but unwilling to give Greek any satisfaction. He finally managed a nod, which was encouragement enough for Greek.

"The cattleman moaned in pain," Greek went on, "and the Moor said as softly as a mother speaking to a baby, 'You're nothing but a damned bully, Deast. And if there's any good law or any good Lord, you'll be brought as low as you deserve. You stay away from Dimon, and you stay away from Coulson or I'll have this puny arm of yours reaching for the surface of the deepest lake in Nebraska.' "

"You saw and heard all of this?" Widlund said.

"I did, sir. Doc and the attorney never moved from their table. Doc sipped his whiskey like he was at a dinner party. The attorney slouched still, as if he didn't want to be discovered. Deast moaned in pain. Then

Jackson let the cattleman's arm down slow and gentle, and he turned Deast around to face him."

Greek turned as if he were the black man and faced Widlund square. He leveled his gaze and paused long to build the moment. Widlund held Greek's stare and waited. When he thought his timing perfect, Greek spoke.

"The cattleman's face was white as a ghost's, sir. The Moor loomed above him, the contrast of their colors as stark as keys on a piano. He stooped to bring his dark face close to Deast, and he tipped his hat and said with no emotion, 'You have a nice day, Mr. Deast.' "

At this point, Greek relaxed his arms and let his shoulders droop, as if he awaited applause. He held his gaze on Widlund, and let the silence fill the scene. When he thought he had let the moment settle just right, he continued in a low voice.

"Then he turned to the silent bunch staring in disbelief, me included. And he said, 'Y'all please keep an eye on this neighbor of yours, will you? His behavior can be uncivilized, and I think he surely can use your help.'

"Then with a slight bow and another tip of his hat, he said,

'Good day, folks.' He left, and it was the quietest moment I've ever heard at the Silver Dollar or anywhere else."

13

Almy's momento

In a few days the air warmed, snow melted away, and spring resumed its noisy arrival. The horses were found alive. They had wandered with the wind but had not foundered. The German neighbor, Francis Schneidermann, whose claim lay to the east beyond the Adams place, found them. With a few inquiries, he figured they belonged to Sutton, and returned them. The cow was healthy and with renewed milking regained her appetite.

Three days later, on Tuesday, the little girl was buried on the high hill northwest of the soddie. Sutton found scrap wood to make a cross. Almy had never used a brace, but Sutton told her how and she bored four holes and used bolts and nuts to fasten the pieces together so it would be sturdy. They worked together to smooth the wood and then Almy carved the inscription as carefully as she could, and Sutton helped. It read, "Viola Sutton, 1901-1907."

There was not enough wood for a burial box, so the neighbors dressed Farmer in her own clothes and wrapped the body in the only wool blanket they had. Almy asked for the handkerchief Farmer usually wore around her neck, and she asked Maddie to tie it in her brown hair. Maddie snugged the bow and then said, "There you are, Viola. You look so pretty today." Almy turned away before her tears betrayed her hurt.

Sutton's hands were too sore to be of much use, so the Adams and Lukasiewicz men dug the grave and made it deep in the sand so the animals could not detect the odor.

When everything was ready, Almy, Maddie and Sutton gathered with the Jay Adams clan, and Jay read the Bible and made short remarks, finishing with "ashes to ashes, dust to dust." He said a prayer, short for him, and he asked all present to have their own silent prayer. Almy whimpered noticeably, and Sutton squeezed her to his side.

Maddie did not cry. She seemed preoccupied with the bright dress she wore, and she turned gaily in it, her arms outstretched and her hands hanging gracefully like a ballerina's. When the ceremony concluded, Adams' wife Elsie tried to talk with her, but Maddie continued to turn in the sunshine, smiling as if she'd just read a pleasant letter from home. Elsie said to her husband in an aside that neither Sutton nor Almy could hear, "I don't know what's wrong with her, Jay."

The Adamses left with little talk, and Maddie, in her first acknowledgement of their presence, waved goodbye. She smiled in a frail manner then wandered off toward the pond, and Sutton went after her.

"Come on home now, Maddie," he said.

He reached for her hand, and she saw the blackened finger tips.

She said, "Will! Put on your gloves or you will freeze."

Sutton moved his arm to her waist and guided her back to the soddie and opened the south door to motion her in. Almy said, "Sit here, Mommy," and Maddie smiled broadly at her then sat and stared through the open door.

* * *

Sutton's fingers were not recovering. At the tip and down past the nails, the fingers on his left hand had turned black. On his right hand, the two stub fingers did not frostbite. From the tips to the cuticles, his fingers were black.

He did not send for the doctor. He knew what would happen. The doctor would amputate them, and the healing might be faster. If he left them to rot, the outcome would be the same; eventually they would fall off, like the umbilical cord of a newborn. For now, there would be no doctor help, and he considered amputating them by himself with a sharpened hatchet from the barn.

More was required of Almy. Her mother was not dependable for any chore. She became more and more distant from Almy and Sutton both. Almy worried and quietly wondered how long it would be before her mother accepted the death of Farmer.

In the community of homesteaders, life gradually returned to normal. On a warm Sunday, Almy, Maddie and Sutton went with the others to community get-together, almost as normal as the other Sand Hills Sundays to which the socially starved families looked forward.

Until Sutton could repair the wagon, they would walk, and so they began. The more fortunate Adamses had a near-new top buggy, and when they overtook the walking Suttons, they offered a ride. There wasn't enough room for all three of them, and Maddie mumbled a refusal anyway. Sutton said he'd stay walking with Maddie, and Almy climbed aboard.

When they had trotted a way ahead, Almy said, "Ma is not herself."

"She's suffered terribly, Almy," Elsie replied as gently as she could. "These things take time to heal. We will all take care of her, and she will get better in time."

Almy rode on in silence and then after a while said, "I miss my sister."

"Of course, you do, dear. And you must never forget her."

Almy, sitting between the two, leaned against Mrs. Adams and the kindly woman stroked Almy's brown hair. Jay slapped the reins against the pony's rump and said, "git on," and the horse trotted.

When the buggy arrived, they helped the Chadwicks with preparations for the get-together. Old man Chadwick and his wife organized the event, as they often did. The women laid out the long table with root vegetables from their cellars. The Petersens brought antelope meat they had only recently taken when a few loner bucks straggled onto their claim. The sun shone brightly on the spacious soddie, and the high windmill, which stood proudly above the muddy and treeless lot, turned in the breeze and the pump creaked the stock tank full with water from the dark reservoirs far below.

More folks arrived by buggy and on foot, bringing their own food. The men were dressed in wool pants and coats, and they wore felt hats. The women wore bonnets and dresses. Some of the men sent the boys to look for wild asparagus shoots by the lake, and the boys came back with fistfuls they bragged about all day. Conversations were subdued at first, but as folks warmed with the food and the spring sunshine, the chatter grew lively.

Maddie sat to the side, and the women tried to include her.

Ida Mae Grim said, "Maddie, won't you have some antelope meat? It's fresh and tasty!"

Maddie moved her lips without saying anything the women could hear.

Almy knelt at her mother's side and said, "Mommy, let's have some meat."

Maddie looked but her vacant eyes were especially wan today. She did not eat. Almy held her mother's hand, but it was lifeless. The smile was gone. Almy took a bite of the meat and said, It's very good, Mommy. Look!

New asparagus, too." But her words brought no response, and Almy gave up.

Sutton sat with Chadwick and the other men. The old man seemed to know the most about folks' troubles. In a matter-of-fact way, he acknowledged that the worst of it in their region was at the Sutton place. There had been loss of livestock, too, he said, and other reports of frostbite. Several of the cattlemen were caught unprepared, and he knew of one up north who lost several hundred head. They were stripping the carcasses to save the meat, and there were so many dead ones that they hauled the bones to the depot in Oshkosh and sent them for rendering in Denver.

Chadwick got a good laugh when he told the story of the man, Nerm Laird, who was nearly caught in the blizzard before he found a soddie. No one was at home, so he went in and made himself comfortable. He was there two days before old Joe Cramer came up from his cyclone cellar, where he and his wife had gone to weather the storm. When they opened the door to their own soddie, there stood Laird wearing one of Mrs. Cramer's calico aprons and a smile from here to Omaha. He said to them, "C'mon in! We never turn a stranger away!"

Through it all Sutton listened quietly, but when the Adamses noticed him stirring at Maddie's side, they offered Almy another ride. This time she said she'd just walk with the family.

"Anything you need, you just holler," Jay Adams said. "Maddie, I'll be bringing some food tomorrow," Elsie said. Maddie did not acknowledge, but Sutton said, "Mighty kind, Mrs. Adams."

It was nearing evening when the Suttons got home. Almy helped her mother out of her coat. Maddie sat quietly at the table, and Almy stoked a fire. Maddie said, Tell Farmer to put on her coat. Almy said, she's gone, Mommy.

"Isn't that her 'kerchief? Why do you have that!? You give it back to her!"

Almy cried, softly at first, but then she covered her face with her hands and ran to her bed, but Maddie did not notice and said nothing apart from the words to the hymn she was softly singing. Sutton went to Almy's side and sat with her on the bed. He tried to think of the right thing to say but words were not easy for him now. He put his right arm around Almy's shoulder and drew her to him, and the sat like that for several minutes. Then he softly folded his left hand into a fist so the fingers wouldn't show and lifted her chin. When her wet eyes met Sutton's, she noticed that her father's eyes were moist, too. She said, "It's all right, Pa." Sutton could only nod as his chin trembled.

He went outside, saying as he opened the door that he'd not be long but had things to do. Almy said, "Sure, Pa," as he rose. She watched him go. Maddie said nothing. Almy dried her eyes and then made herself busy in the hut.

Outside, the snow had melted into the sand, and the pond teemed with waterfowl. Sutton went there and was alone with a mountain of thoughts and emotions that he had buried deep inside. He thought he should not have allowed himself any sorrow. Not only was Maddie not herself, but Almy needed to know she could depend on her strong father, but now at the pond and back there a few minutes ago in the hut, he didn't feel strong.

The pond seemed tranquil where he stood. He tried to make some sense of all that had happened. He put the sequence of events into his mind and played them again and again, and each time it came out the same. When he considered what must be done tomorrow and the next day, he didn't know the answers.

In the reeds, he saw an antelope skull, and he picked it up, examining it for some locked truth. The skull of his own small daughter lay in the

Nebraska sand, and his own skull would someday lie in the hills, too, maybe buried deep like Farmer or maybe just blown over with sand. He held the skull oddly in his two palms. He looked into the eye sockets and turned the skull to study the upper jaw and its remaining teeth. At the top, the horns protruded as they did before the death rotted away the flesh and left only this horned skull of a pronghorn, in his estimation the most majestic of the wild animals that remained on the prairie.

It annoyed him, being alone with this remnant of an animal. This creature, pushed along by a great force, yielding to the natural order of things, as all do. God or nature, he wasn't sure, intended life in this harsh country to be this way. He did not want to think of death, so he held the skull at eye level and pictured the buck silhouetted on a high sand hill against a rising sun. To see it so in his mind was preferable than the acknowledgement that, magnificent or not, the buck had come to a muddy grave.

He stooped and in the cold pondwater washed the mud from the eye sockets. With a reed, he picked the teeth clean. In the water, he swished the skull again, and the last of the mud swirled away in a soupy brown pool. When he lifted the skull, the sun glistened on the wetted bone.

He carried the skull to the barn and wiped it dry with an old piece of burlap. He found a board, and despite the ache in his knuckles, hammered in the nails. Using a spike which he held clumsily in his fist, he scratched "Bold Buck 1907. R.I.P."on the board just below the gaping upper jaw.

He placed the old ladder above the entry to the barn where the timber lintel was situated to hold the sod above. With a single nail, he hung the board, then climbed down to see how it looked. When he realized it sagged to the left, he vowed he would level it later.

<u>14</u>

'She weren't right'

Doc finished up in the early afternoon and went to the store before stopping for a drink. Ruthie Kremlacek and her husband were there, and Ruthie was making the rounds with everything she knew or had heard. The worst of it, she said, was Maddie Sutton. She'd lost a child and it pushed her over the edge. Lost her youngest. Lost the little Viola, but six years old. So hard.

When the Doc overheard, he said to Ruthie, "What do you mean?"

Standing in the grocery, Ruthie said,

"Well, Doc, she weren't right."

Doc asked for more.

"Well, her nerves a' breaking down, Doc. She's talking to voices she hears. She don't recognize her own family. Doc, you need to see her."

Doc said they should get her to town. Sometimes people like this are dangerous, he said. They can snap. They see things that aren't real, and if they start to believe their own stories, they can get nasty. He'd seen it before, and people like that just needed to be sent away so they can get the proper care and the family and neighbors will be safe.

Hearing that, others gathered around and listened intently. "What would Sutton do without her?" Ruthie asked.

"Well, now, Mr. Sutton is a strong man, isn't he? We need to ask another question, Mrs. Kremlacek, and it's this: What's he going to do with her?" Doc said.

"Why Doc, that's frightful," she said. "That'd leave Almy with the load of work."

"Lot of girls out here do just fine at that age, Mrs. Kremlacek. They're ready. They need to know a thing or two when they're young and ripe like her, if they hope to do any good out here," he said.

Some of the men agreed, and the women, including Ruthie, were quiet.

Doc smiled as he made a curious twist to his bushy mustache and paused as if thinking. Then he said, "How's Mr. Sutton doing?" and Ruthie thought it was a normal question of neighborly concern with nothing else in Doc's mind. Ruthie chatted on.

"Oh, he's sufferin', that's for sure, Doc. A passel of worries on that man's mind," she said.

Widlund walked in and saw the crowd around Doc and Ruthie. When they saw him, they became quiet and watched cautiously as he moved into the crowd.

"Mornin,' everyone," he said. He took it in with quick glances.

"Everyone seen a ghost? Or is this just an apparition I'm seeing? We've lost our way in this sea of white?" he asked with a wry smile. Doc stepped forward and extended his hand.

"Good morning, Mr. Editor. Ruthie here has some news. I'm sorry, sir."

Widlund fingered the lapels of his coat and adjusted his stance. He looked from eye to eye around the circle that had gathered. He read the faces and knew the news somehow affected him personally. His thoughts went to Mildred, but he had only just left her; she could have no trouble. Then Sutton. Could it be Sutton?

"What news?" he said. Ruthie lowered her head and looked toward Doc. She found her husband's eyes and wondered what he would suggest. She turned to Widlund and studied his puzzled face. He shifted his weight with impatience and when he did, she spoke.

"Charles, the Suttons have had trouble from this storm," she said.

Her husband stepped to her side and took Ruthie's arm.

"They've lost their youngest to the storm," he said.

Widlund could not absorb the information. Youngest? Viola?

"She's dead, Charles. She wandered off and got stuck outside. They found her in a drift," Emil Kremlacek said.

Doc stepped forward and with his left hand took Widlund's arm as if offering comfort. He stroked his mustache with the pink fingers of his right hand and said, "We've heard that his wife, his dear wife, is not taking it so well. Perhaps you should go. She should be brought in for evaluation."

"Evaluation?" Widlund said.

"Well, Charles," Ruthie confessed, "She's a'hearin' voices, they say."

"Hearing voices," he said. "Is that so? And this information comes from … ?"

"The Adamses have been with 'em, Charles. There was a little service for her. Jay was there. He helped dig the grave. He said Maddie isn't handling it well. Doc here thinks she ought to be evaluated, because she might need help from the mental doctors," Emil said.

Widlund thanked them. He backed away slowly, thanked them all again, and left.

"If I can help … " he heard the Doc offer as he hurried away.

15

Almy catches the fever

DOC BRONSON was busy from the storm, and a damn good thing we've got him, someone said. At the edge of town, the old spinster Millie Foster had stoked her furnace and then packed newspapers around the windows and doors. The house filled with smoke, and the old lady was nearly overcome. She pushed open her door, and in her nightclothes ran screaming to the neighbors. Not so nimble anymore, she tangled in her gown and fell to the ground, where she lay moaning. No one heard her, and the sharp cold pressed into her limbs quickly, so she forced herself to rise and get to the neighbor's door. She was so cold already that the neighbors thought she would die. Someone went for the Doc, and he came to the house with his bag and advised them to get her out of her wet nightgown first, and he cussed under his breath when he said so, but no one heard his indictment of their lack of common sense. Then the Doc instructed them to warm blankets by the fire and change them one after the other tightly around her. He said a sip of whiskey would help, too, if anyone had any, but no one said they did.

As she warmed up, she seemed to be disoriented, and when the neighbors talked to her she would stare vacantly into the bare window and ask about Minnie Marie. Nobody knew who she was talking about, until one of the women said, "Why, that's her little twin sister that died." She said years ago Millie told some of the ladies about her sister's death on the early homestead up by Fort Robinson, and she said it was a hard time, because Minnie Marie died in Millie's arms as her mother prepared a poultice. She said the doctor blamed the scarlet fever. But no one ever heard her talk about it again.

When she got hysterical, they sent for Doc Bronson again, and this time he didn't come. He sent a message to them that they'd have to bring her into the office, because he was too busy to come there. When they got her there, the Doc was too busy to see her right away and she sat in the waiting area talking loudly to her dead sister, and everyone looked the other way and shook their heads. Finally, Doc Bronson called her in, and the others waited. They heard her yammering away, and then suddenly there was a loud smack and a yell from Millie, then whimpering only. When the Doc brought Millie to the door and stood at her side for someone to fetch her, he wore a satisfied smile as if he had applied his best medicine. The people in the waiting area were surprised at his look, because they expected the Doc to be concerned and a little saddened by his patient's state, but instead he wore a smile and said only, Next.

Almy and Elsie Adams waited, too, and hoped they would be called soon. But the old banker Gates rose and went in, limping and making grunts and groans with each step. Almy and Elsie looked at the old man and then smiled at each other as he creaked along in elderly pain.

Almy did not know why she was in the doctor's office. She worried that she should not be away from her mother. Mrs. Adams sat with her and occasionally reached for her hand when Almy would sob. Almy wore her dress, and as she did every day now, she tied Farmer's white handkerchief around her neck, and its bright red embroidered strawberries seemed festive for a doctor's office.

She had not felt well, and she hadn't slept much since that awful day. When the night was at its darkest and the hut was altogether quiet except for the mice that scurried across the dirt floor, dark dreams visited Almy and she would sit straight up in bed, fearful and sobbing. Her mother's restlessness disturbed her as well. Maddie's throaty moan was sadly dark, and Almy would lie alone and think that her mother might need something that she could get for her. And when Maddie screamed in the night, Almy would hear the twisted dream words and to her it sounded as if her mother were saying, "Stay down," but when Almy became fully awake and thought about it with her senses tuned, she couldn't be sure what her mother had screamed. She would listen intently and sometimes hear Sutton whisper, "Shhh, Maddie. It's all right, dear." Sometimes she heard Sutton rustle in the bed and there would be rhythmic creaks. She would hear her mother moan and Sutton's breathing heavier, and she hoped it would be better for her mother. Then it would be difficult for her to get back to sleep, and sometimes the spring day would dawn, and she would wonder if she had slept at all.

Then the day's work would begin. Pa would want coffee, and she would explain again that all they had was alfalfa tea, and she would stoke a fire and heat the water for him. He would sit with Maddie, but when Sutton would ask a question, Maddie would often not respond at all, but sometimes she would say something, but it wouldn't relate to his question. Then Sutton would rise quietly and go outside where a dozen chores greeted him, and he responded listlessly.

Left in the hut with her mother, Almy did her best to make things pleasant. She smiled broadly and hummed as she busied herself. When her mother would say something strange and disconnected, Almy would smile and softly tell her mother that she understood. The most hurtful moments and the ones Almy took to bed with her happened when Maddie would seem to speak not to her but to her deceased sister. Then Almy would cry inaudibly, and if she couldn't hide her distress, she would slip to the root cellar, bury her head in her apron, and sob until her grief passed.

Mrs. Adams had become especially concerned for her. When she visited, as she tried to do often, she would encourage Almy to talk, and she paid attention to the child, and attended to her words. A sensitive woman, she spoke softly and positively. So, when Almy's color changed and when her conversation would become oddly repetitive, she suspected that the child's spirits were down. She made teas and brought oils for Almy to take, but the child lost weight and talked less. She thought a visit to the doctor was necessary, so she asked Sutton if she and Jay could perhaps take Almy with them on their trip to Rackett for supplies. Confused, Sutton dashed his gaze from Almy to Maddie and then back to Mrs. Adams, and without understanding the urgency of Almy's needs simply said yes to Mrs. Adams, and Almy went along.

Suddenly Doc Bronson opened the door and the old banker grunted from the Doc's examination office and into the waiting area. In front of the waiting patients, he buttoned his pants and then awkwardly went out the door. Doc looked directly at Almy and said Next and she looked apprehensively at Mrs. Adams. The kindly neighbor squeezed Almy's hand again and told her not to be afraid and to go with the doctor.

The strange examining room was surprisingly warm to her. She noticed the decorative wallpaper and stood wide-eyed with wonder at its gaudy formality. She had never seen anything like it. The doctor's desk was imposing to her, and his formidable bookcases seemed to loom above her with distinction and bold appeal. Her attention went quickly to the doctor's books, and when she scanned the titles, she was curious. She searched for anything recognizable but could only wonder if the books were for doctors only.

When the Doc saw her interest, he took down his anatomy book and opened it casually to the colored drawings of stomach, arm and leg muscles. When she looked more closely, the Doc leafed through the pages until he came to the drawings of female breasts and genitalia, and Almy looked away shyly. The doctor said in a soft voice, "It's just the female body, Almy. Don't be afraid." Bronson watched her turn her eyes again to the drawings, and after a moment he said, "Look here at this." He turned the pages to the drawings of the male parts and Almy again turned away in embarrassment. He placed his fingers on her shoulder and said, "And this is the male part. Nothing to be afraid of." She paused and looked up the doctor. He looked down on her with a smile she did not understand.

He said, "Here, little dear. Sit here on this table" and Almy did as he said. He closed the book and returned it to the shelf, then said gently, "What brings you in, darling?"

Almy swallowed and tried to find her voice. Meekly, she said, "My mother isn't well."

"And how do you feel about that?"

Almy didn't know what he could mean. She said, "She thinks sometimes that I'm not me. That I'm my sister. My sister is dead."

"Your mother is very sad. You must be brave. Do you eat well?"

"I'm not very hungry."

"Do you sleep well at night?"

"Sometimes."

"Let's have a feel of your temperature."

He placed the back of his hand on her brow, and as he did her innocent eyes lifted so she could look into the doctor's face.

He said hmm and I see.

Then he said, "We will need to take your temperature. I think you have a fever."

"What's that?" she said.

"We don't want your body to get too hot. We want it to be normal. Let's have a look."

He told her to lie on her stomach and lift her dress and pull down her underwear, and she did as he said. Then he went to his medicine case and returned with the thermometer and inserted it. As he did, he said, "You will feel a little tickle, but it's all right." She didn't know what the feeling was, but she lay still. The doctor placed his hands on her back, and she felt the cold fingers when he moved one to her buttocks. As he waited, he said, the doctor will take good care of you, and soon you will feel better. He removed the thermometer, and said, my dear beautiful girl, you have a fever. You are too hot, and we must cool you.

"Please remove your clothing and lie on your back."

She did as he said, but she asked if she could leave Farmer's handkerchief around her neck, and he said, "Why, of course! It looks very lovely there, doesn't it? Are those strawberries?"

"Yes. It was my sister's."

The doctor went to his cabinet again and returned with a folded white sheet. He rolled a wooden frame to the examination table and positioned it so that it made an arc above Almy when she lay on her back.

Then he draped the sheet over the screen. He placed the frame so that Almy's lower body was blocked from her view. Then he knelt and began to turn something she could hear. As he did Almy could feel her hips lift and her legs move lower. The doctor rose from his kneeling position and placed himself at the foot of the examination table, and Almy could see his head and shoulders above the white sheet. He adjusted his body so that he was closer to her head, then she watched his head disappear behind the white sheet. Then he stood again and moving again to the side of the table adjusted it some more. Where her legs lay, the table was divided, and she could feel the two pieces move apart as the doctor turned the cranks underneath. Then he positioned himself between the leg rests and said there, there that's better.

Then he explained in a breathy voice that he would examine her again, and she should not worry if she felt just a little pain. She studied him carefully and noticed that his wool suit coat had vertical stripes in white that made him look tall. He wore a bow tie that was neatly pulled tight to his white neck, and it was brown, like dried grass in the winter. She carefully studied his brown mustache and she was glad she did not have hair on her face like this doctor. She felt a tickle as if the doctor were brushing something there, and she thought it must be the instrument he said he would use to cool her. The doctor then pressed it against her, and she could feel something hard enter her and then she felt a sharp pain and she said ouch!

The doctor said he was sorry, but sometimes this could hurt a little bit, but she should not worry. He smiled when he said these words, and she thought he was being very kind. He closed his eyes and seemed to move forward and backward, and Almy felt the instrument move inside her, and the pain seemed to go away. She watched the doctor's face again, and his eyes seemed to roll into their sockets, and he exhaled as if he had just let go of something heavy. Then he slowly backed away from his position and adjusted the sheet because it had slipped down toward the table. He turned his back to her, and all she could see was the brown coat with its white stripes on his broad shoulders. He stood like that for a few moments, adjusting his clothing. Then he walked to the medicine case again and returned to her with a small vial which she could see above the sheet. He held it to the light and examined it closely, then held a cloth to its opening and tipped it so that the liquid inside poured out in a small amount that was yellow against the white cloth. Then he stooped down, and she could no longer see his head, and then she felt a cool liquid. The pain she had felt there went away immediately, and he asked if she felt all right.

"Yes," she said.

He removed the sheet and dabbed her with the corner of it, and when he lifted it away, she could see the yellow spots on it, and there was red, too. She thought it looked like blood, as if she had cut her finger and used the sheet to stop the bleeding, but she didn't think she had been cut.

The doctor said don't worry, darling. There will be a little pain, and maybe some blood. It's normal. But now the thermometer says you are quite well, and if you eat well, get a good night's sleep and do your chores so you father and mother love you more, you will be a healthy and happy young woman.

She sat naked on the examination table and the doctor extended his hand to help her down. He told her she could put her clothes back on in a minute, but before she did he wanted to ask if he could see the handkerchief she wore. Then he turned it so the knot was at the front, and he untied it. Then he stepped back and looked at her carefully, up and down. She stood naked without a movement, her arms hanging limply at her sides and her eyes doleful.

"You are a good patient, and I want to ask you a very special favor, may I?"

"Yes"

"I would like to have this scarf. May I keep it? May I have it here to remind me of you and your sister?"

Almy was confused. She could not understand why the doctor would want the handkerchief, except that he would want to remember Farmer as she did. She remembered that her mother didn't like her to have the handkerchief anyway and always called her Viola when she wore it. If she didn't have it anymore, she couldn't wear it and maybe then her mother wouldn't snap at her. She nodded her approval.

He said, "Thank you dear," and then looking lower, he said, "Oh, dear. There's a small drop. Let me clean that."

He used the handkerchief and daubed the trickle away. Her blood, darker red than the strawberries, sickened her, but she stood against her fear and said nothing. The handkerchief lay in the doctor's open hand, and she touched it gently as if to say goodbye, then looked up to the doctor.

When their eyes met, she blinked the tear away as she said, "Please keep it for me."

16

Widlund gets the story

WHEN THE door opened, Mrs. Adams rose and waited for Almy to come to her. The Doc, more interested than usual, walked with Almy to Mrs. Adams and spoke in a friendly, concerned voice.

"You were quite correct to bring her in, Mrs. Adams. She is running a fever, and I think we have brought her temperature to normal. She isn't sleeping well, and she has lost her appetite. But you are feeling better now, aren't you?"

Almy said nothing. She moved her cheerless eyes from Mrs. Adams to the doctor.

Doc Bronson said, "Mrs. Adams, I should see Maddie. Will you speak to her husband?"

Mrs. Adams examined the doctor's face, thinking it was odd that he would bring that up now. But he was right; Maddie should see the doctor, and perhaps there was something he could do for her. If she could perhaps take the proper medicine or have the proper counsel, things would go so much easier for the Suttons. She thought the decision wasn't hers. That it should be up to Sutton. Approaching that subject on her own may not go well. She wondered if her husband could help. Then she thought of Widlund, and spoke to the doctor, "I will stop next door and talk with Charles about that, Doctor."

"I don't know that you need to talk to him," the doctor said.

Almy said, "I will talk to Pa."

When she said it Doc Bronson's eyebrows raised, and he turned suddenly to her. He studied her face for betrayal, and his hard look nearly became a glare before he checked himself. Mrs. Adams didn't see. His look frightened Almy, and when the Doc saw only fear, he relaxed. Smiled.

"You are right, young lady. Ask your Pa if he doesn't think your mother should come and see the doctor."

"Pa's fingers are bad. You can make them better?"

"He has 'em frostbit, doesn't he? We should look at them."

Mrs. Adams said, "Maddie so sad, Sutton with frostbite, and this child with a fever. Trouble is no stranger to this land. Thank you, Doctor Bronson."

She took Almy's hand, and they walked into the sunlit boardwalk. Mrs. Adams paused to look up and down the muddy main street, then said, "Why it's a beautiful day, isn't it, Almy?"

They walked hand in hand to the next door, and Widlund greeted them warmly when they entered.

"Almy! Come here, my child!"

Reserved but happy, Almy hugged her uncle.

"Hello, Mrs. Adams. Very nice to see you. It looks as if the sun hasn't entirely forgotten us," he said. "Almy, I have a book for you, dear. It isn't Crusoe, as you hoped, but I think you'll like Mr. Twain. His humor is profound. And for pleasure only, a spanking-new volume of the poems by Robert W. Service. Good one, this, Almy. Enjoy it!"

"Thank you, Uncle Charles," she said.

The leather bindings warmed in her hands, and she leafed through the illustrated pages of Tom Sawyer with great interest.

"Please sit down," he said, clearing a stack of newspapers from the two chairs by his desk. Widlund wondered why it was Mrs. Adams who was here with Almy.

"Where's Sutton? And Maddie?"

"Ma is home," Almy said.

Widlund looked into her eyes for information. No smile.

"How is your Pa?" he asked.

"He's fine, 'cept his fingers."

Mrs. Adams shifted in the chair. "He got a terrible frostbite, Charles. Some of the fingers don't look so good. I told Doc. Maybe we can get him in to see Doc. He's stubborn."

"Pa's not stubborn," Almy protested.

"Doc thinks he should see Maddie, too."

When they left, Widlund decided it was time to get to the homestead. Mildred had urged him to go, but he delayed because of his overwhelming workload. Now it was time; they would go as soon as they could.

17

The Widlunds visit

WIDLUND TENSED the reins and coaxed the gelding around the wash. The top buggy sloshed through the still-muddy low road, Widlund's preferred route to Sutton's homestead. It was longer this way, but he liked the lakes, especially Crescent Lake, which teemed this time of year with migrating waterfowl. Mildred, at his side, worried that her sister was in trouble. Together they rode in comfortable silence.

His mind raced. Follow up on the Tomppert entry. Was that a widow entry? Or was it a legitimate Kincaider who somehow got into and out of trouble in such a short time? Something not right there. Deast manipulating an entry? Different topic: How will Sutton react? Maddie having a nervous breakdown? What's Sutton going to do? Worried about Almy. Too much for a little girl, but she's a smart one. Different topic: Who's this settler with courage to stand up to Deast? Asking for trouble. Black man? More invitation for trouble.

Tomppert entry. Female claim. Plenty of women among the claimants for federal land; this one suspicious. Who challenged it? Maybe the claim borders one of Deast's coveted grazing lands? Deast make a claim in the name of a widow or resident of some old soldier's home in Omaha or Hastings? He'd seen it before. Erect a shack, have a surrogate occupy it for a night every six months and then claim the requirements of the act had been fulfilled. Easy enough to pay off the widows or elderly soldiers, and very easy to persuade most of them that the land was better used by cattlemen, if an explanation were needed at all. In the worst case, if the government should reject the claim as fraudulent, then it was easy enough to stall by appeal to the Interior department and continue to fence and use the claim in the meantime. There was no shortage of men with their own ideas about the west to help Deast and his ilk collaborate. Hell, most of the newspapers tipped their hats to the cattle interests. For that matter, who could show that this forsaken country could support a farmer? Could Sutton or the neighbors make something of it? Maybe, if hard times would leave 'em alone, but for now it's a hard time for Sutton. Poor man's got a sea of sand and an ocean of problems out here.

What of Sutton's own claim? Maybe Deast was after it, too. The way this Kincaid law was written, Deast or one of his men could keep an eye on Sutton, and if anything could be shown to challenge his entry, they'd be the first in line to take it for themselves. And, if, as he began to suspect, the Tomppert claim was near or adjacent to Sutton's, the motive for Deast to grab the contingent entries would be even greater. He'd heard of some trouble in the area, but not from Sutton himself. His brother-in-law was not one to holler for help. And what of this black man? Did Sutton know anything of him? Damn, he hated to bring up land fraud and the dirty dealings of some of the cattlemen, when Sutton's plate of troubles was full enough. Still, he resolved to look for an opportunity to talk.

He drove the buggy on, thinking what a fine day it was. Thinking. This land -- oh, this land. Unpredictable. Horrible storm a few weeks ago now; now a pleasant spring day with all the anticipation and hope a cloudless sky could bring. Bench grass whisked in the breeze, the old blades rattling like forgotten sabers, and the soft shoots pushing from below. And there, between the clumps of grass, the sand waited expectantly, like pods of travelers waiting for a heavy train. Overhead, cranes beaked their cries, waves of them northbound for breeding grounds more hospitable than these hostile old sand hills. Waterfowl followed the changing weather as if under orders. A lone antelope appeared on the hill ahead, its form silhouetted black against the clear sky. Somewhere the yearlings munched the grass shoots under the does' protection, all of them bulking up after a demanding winter. In town once, an early homesteader said the elk still roamed when he and his wife built their soddie on wild land north of Rackett, but Widlund hadn't seen elk. Those animals, along with the bison, had been decimated and then eliminated. Although it was impossible to see at times, the land was giving in to the persistence of human newcomers. Even the gray wolves, feared by all the early 'steaders and methodically hunted by the cattlemen, had disappeared. The land is yielding to the heavy demands of humans, Widlund thought. Except for its weather, the land was more and more under control.

If these natural opponents fit into some broad category of evil, they were subdued. Evil driven out; good at the ready. A tamed place, where men and women could raise their children, grow their food, steward their land, be social when they cared to be, and live a life as good as any garden of Eden. Only the people and the weather caused trouble. No solution for the weather. How to rid the land of evil people? How to subdue the conquest of rivals? How to entrench justice, order? Rule of law?

So Widlund's mind wandered as the buggy rocked to the rhythmic clop of the gelding's hooves. He looked at Mildred and stared so appreciatively that she turned in recognition and smiled faintly. He returned the look with no parting of his lips, just a pencil line smile that she read completely.

This companion, this woman; he deeply loved her but could put no words to it, didn't need to. Dependable and incapable of evil. He looked imploringly into her brown eyes, quietly marveling at the multi-hued shafts that burst from her black pupils, drawn tightly in the bright sun.

"Mildred," he said, "I am thinking ... that story you were reading to me in Blackwood's ... it was about some evil man, do you recall?"

"Charles! I thought you were awfully quiet for this lonesome ride. Your mind ... always busy. Is it the paper?"

What could be said about her? Beautiful? He always thought so. Quiet? When she needed to be. Demure? Supportive? Consistent? Strong? Yes; all of these. But more: Her mind. Playful? Yes. Thoughtful? Always. Challenging? Yes. In the good way, as if he had a reserve, a backup. She kept her judgment at the ready, and offered it when requested, and then with a balanced, seldom judgmental, tone. He did not think of himself as brilliant, regarding Mildred's intellect more highly, stimulated always by her extensive reading. He believed that when his mind was racing, as it was now, she could initiate pause and then redirect his thinking in ways that built on their collective cognition. When his emotions got the better of his thinking, she provided calm consideration.

"This country is made of hard-working people. The land and the elements are adversaries -- tough ones. But the people I sometimes think, Mildred, are more dangerous than the elements. Do you think ... are there bad people and good people?" The buggy jerked sharply, and Widlund pitched into Mildred's shoulder. She yelped, "Hey!" and Widlund sheepishly apologized, as if he were to blame. There in a buggy's lurch was a symbol of all he loved about her: A jolt of good sense when he needed it. He snapped from his thoughts as if slapped and felt ashamed for his lack of sensitivity. It was, after all, Mildred's own sister who was in trouble. Her own niece whom the storm had taken. He sat stiffly upright and concentrated on the reins.

Aware, she answered. He could barely hear her airy voice above the swish of the grass, the clop of the hooves, the creak of the buggy's sandy axle.

"Of course, Charles. Of course. We struggle against them, and within ourselves as well. There are evil men and women who refuse all rules. They hear of taboo and invite it in. They are few who give in to it thoroughly. I wonder if the elements of both good and evil are there inside each of us. If all were good, there would be no Shakespeare, no Shelley, no confessional. Hamlet would not equivocate. No one would qualify for Milton's lost paradise. Maybe evil is not as worrisome as the unwillingness to stand against it. We each do battle, don't we?"

They passed the lake and listened intently as the waterfowl unleashed a chorus of varied song. The water, set against the golden grasses, was as blue as topaz. No tree grew here, even with the steady supply of water and nutrients. In these hills, only grass, reeds, water, and sand are spread copiously under an endless sky. With these sights before him, his mind went to work again. He imagined a blank canvas, white and empty. He splashed pigments with proper names, such as indigo and cobalt and cerulean -- the deepest and most complete hues he could imagine, spread horizontally to make his imagined lake. Then he pictured vertical patches of permanent yellow and ochre and Indian yellow daubed vaguely above and around the blue lake. Then his mind spread ultramarine across the top and let it lay precariously over the rest. He played with the image, arranging it mentally, silently acknowledging his inability with art and drawing. If he were an artist, like a friend he once had, his impression of this broad land would begin with such blobs of color lacking definition and heavy. It would be here among color masses that the people of this land would labor, and if he were good with brush and pen, he would ink them in with intense detail. Only in the upper left, where eye movement begins, would he place the darkest colors, and this amorphous shape would represent the insidious threats this land harbored. There would be no definition to it, and it would hang from nothing and appear poised to fall arbitrarily.

She said, "The article you mention was by a new writer. He speaks several languages but writes in English. He places his evil character in a jungle at the head of a river in Africa. I think that's the one you mean. I do not recall his name. His character was very evil but not well defined. He was described by a sailor who had experienced him."

Then she said, "Oh, I just had a wonderful realization, Charles! Isn't it wonderful that out here in this dusty and untamed land we can stay current with magazines sent by mail? We are so fortunate, so very fortunate."

He fell silent. He thought it insightful of her to juxtapose at this moment the civilized writers of Europe and the developing new world to which they had come. The buggy poked along, the rhythm of its wheels soothing as a baby's cradle. The conversation wilted as each of them drifted into their own thoughts.

Soon the familiar hill above the Sutton hut was visible, and then came the turn into the tiny valley, the sod barn and hut straight ahead, the pond behind. The homestead lay quiet. No dog barked; no horse neighed. The Widlunds moved quietly into the area between the south door and the barn, and Charles pulled the buggy to a stop.

They sat with no sound and looked about. At the window, Mildred saw something. She held her gaze there, searching. A face, wan and blank, slowly disappeared to the side of the glazing then reappeared just as slowly. A woman. She held a cloth to her forehead, and it fell partially across her nose. Mildred could see now, and she brought her hand to her mouth, which dropped open. She whispered, "Charles ..."

Widlund looked at Mildred and caught the direction of her gaze. He followed it to the window and saw the face of his sister- in-law, barely recognizable. His hand loosed the reins, and the horse shifted slightly. He reached for Mildred's hand and gripped it with reassurance. She squeezed back. The door opened, and Almy, gaunt and hesitant, came out.

"Hello, Aunt Mildred. Hello Uncle Charles," she said.

The Widlunds nodded and managed smiles. They climbed down from the seat and ran to Almy and hugged her. Almy felt limp and frail, and they wondered if she had eaten. Charles put his hand under her chin and lifted her face. Mildred saw, too, and put both arms around the girl and hugged her again. She stroked her hair and was aware of the oil and dirt and tangles in it. She rubbed the girl's shoulders and back, and Almy squeezed back.

From inside the hut came a yell.

"Get Farmer inside. She'll freeze out there! Tell those people to go away!"

Almy said, "Yes, mother."

She looked at her aunt and when Mildred took her face between her hands, she began to sob. Large tears poured down her cheeks and left crooked white trails where the dirt was washed. Mildred took her hanky from her pocket and mopped the girl's face and caressed it gently. She took Almy's small shoulders and squared them, then dropped her hands along Almy's hanging arms to her hands and squeezed them both before lifting them in unison and holding them to her lips and kissing them again and again.

Widlund stood with his arms limp. He heard steps behind him and turned. His brother-in-law walked across the yard from the barn, his hands clinched slightly to hide the black tips. The men surveyed each other up and down. Widlund searched Sutton's face and saw a different man. He extended his right hand to shake, but Sutton folded his arms cautiously to his ribs.

Sutton said, "By God, Charles it's good to see you. Come in." Then he pulled close to Widlund's ear and said, "Maddie's having a time of it, Charles. Can't be sure she'll welcome ya."

Widlund said, "We want to help, Will."

Almy looked to her father and then to Mildred and back. Sutton put his arm on her shoulder and turned her to the door. From behind, Widlund saw the black tips of Sutton's right hand, then looked to his left hand as it hung to his side, and he could see the black there, too. The nails were lifeless yellow, like wet sand, and behind them the flesh gradually turned normal.

Inside, Maddie sat on the bench by the south window, from where she had peeked. She still held the cloth, and they could see it was a ragged piece of a flour sack. She was motionless and said nothing. Her eyes darted anxiously from Widlund to Mildred and back. Mildred spoke.

"Maddie, dear. How nice to see you. How are you? May I sit here?"

She moved to her sister as she spoke, and Maddie bent away and turned her face down.

"It's me, Maddie. Your sister. Mildred."

Maddie looked up vacantly and said, "Have you brought Farmer?"

The whole hut was silent. Sutton looked at Mildred and wondered what she would do. He wanted to remove her. He wanted to remove Almy and Charles and himself and go to a pleasant place by the pond.

"Dear sister. We will help you find her. We will need your help. You must eat and sleep and make yourself as healthy as you can. This family will find each other always, won't we? Now, you take my hand, and we are going to walk to the pond and back. There are new ducks to see. Now come."

To Sutton's surprise Maddie rose and took Mildred's hand. "You come with us, Almy. Let's have a walk."

The three of them moved slowly to the door. Maddie's steps were halting, unsure. Almy offered her own hand, but Maddie looked sternly at her and rejected it. The child turned away, but Mildred said, "Come along, Almy," and she did as her aunt directed.

Widlund and Sutton stood in the room. Widlund said, "Will, you need to see Doc Bronson. Those fingers are not going to hold. He can get 'em healthy."

Sutton said, "I've already lost a couple to the rake, Charles. I guess I'm a stubber. I'll get along."

"You think about it, Will. You let 'em rot off and it will take months. Let Doc cut, and they'll be healing, and you can get to your chores."

"I'm worried about Maddie. She's not much with us, Charles. Sits and worries, except when she is mean to Almy."

"Let's get her to town, Will. She will do better if she can have Mildred to help her. You and her and Almy stay with us until things clear. Neighbors can look after the animals. You come with us."

Sutton stood quietly. His head hung, then he squared his shoulders and firmed his stance.

"I need to do something, Charles. This ain't working right now."

18

The insanity board meets

THE ADAMSES came for the animals. They pastured the horses and cow and kept a stall in the barn for milking. Kremlaceks came for Sutton, Maddie and Almy. Sutton put the place in order, with Almy's help, and they left for the Widlunds place in town.

Over the course of the next few days, Maddie began to talk more with Mildred, moving away from the dark inner space to which she had retreated. Almy read her aunt and uncle's books when she could, but was more interested in her mother's progress and her aunt's consistent loving way. The three of them tilled a garden in the little plot outside the Widlund house. For lunch each day, they prepared hearty meals of beef or pork lavished with buttery gravies and last year's potatoes mashed in cream and butter and tended with carrots.

Sutton puttered around town or read. His frostbitten fingers shriveled grotesquely and began the slow process of sloughing away. Widlund pressed him to see Doc Bronson, but he stalled. He preferred to spend his time around town, and occasionally stopped at the Silver Dollar where he would sit with the men and talk about the land. His fingers were a topic with everyone, and he had begun to enjoy the reactions when folks gasped at the sight of them. If a newcomer happened along, he would hide them coyly as he waited for an opportunity. Then, as he began a somber soliloquy on some obscure topic, he would raise an index finger as if to make a point, then burst into laughter when the listener gasped.

At lunch one day, Widlund said, "You get those fingers fixed, Will. Speed up this process so you can get back."

"You're tired of me already, brother?"

"Now, dammit -- excuse me, Mildred -- Will, don't go that way on me. You'll do better to get on with it."

Sutton sat straight up, his back ramrodded against the chair back. He used his fork awkwardly, like a child. He jabbed at his meat and when he tried to couple his next bite with the potatoes, he lost his clumsy hold and the fork squirted from his hand and the food splashed to the tablecloth.

"I guess you're on to something there, Charles," he said drily. He gripped his cup with both hands as he and Charles sipped coffee and Mildred and Maddie cleared the table. There came a loud knock on the door. Widlund answered, and there stood Jason Buck, wearing a grim look.

"Charles, I am here to say that we need to have Mrs. Sutton report to the courthouse this afternoon. "

Widlund looked at him with suspicion. Buck stood on the porch, waiting for an invitation to enter. It did not come. Widlund said, "Why would you need that, Jason?"

"Townsfolk are concerned, Charles. The board will have a look and make its own assessment," he said.

"Board?"

"Insanity Board, Charles. There are concerns."

"She's doing better, Jason. There's no need for any alarm."

"That's why we have the insanity board, Charles. We will have a look. If she's fine, then there will be no need for any action. Townsfolk must be protected."

"She lost a child, sir. For heaven's sake."

Sutton heard the conversation. He moved slowly to the door and searched Buck's face without speaking. Widlund angled himself so the two stood together to face Buck. Sutton said, "You're standing on Mr. Widlund's front porch. This here's my brother-in-law. I'm getting the idea he don't want you here."

Buck said, "We can do this any way you like. We can come get her, or you can bring her to the courthouse this afternoon. The sheriff has been notified. He will come for her if you don't bring her. The time is 3 o'clock. We will expect to see you then."

He left the porch and closed the yard gate as he left. Sutton and Widlund watched him go. Said nothing.

* * *

The Insanity Board met in the basement of the courthouse, down a flight of stone steps and through a narrow hall with pipes running along the ceiling. A wooden door stood ajar, and Sheriff Mike Brier pushed it open for Widlund, Sutton, and Maddie to enter. Inside were four men. One sat near the center of a small table, and three others sat in chairs, flanking the man in the middle. There were four empty chairs facing the seated men. At the table was Doc Bronson. To his left were Deast and a cattleman named Yi Yi Jorgensen. To his right was Buck. Sheriff Brier sat in the remaining chair, removed his hat, and placed it in his lap. His sheriff's badge was pinned to a leather vest, his pistol strapped to his hip. Doc Bronson opened the top buttons of his woolen coat and shuffled in his seat for comfort. He leaned slightly back and grinned.

"Maddie, it is nice to see you again. Hello, Mr. Sutton. Mr. Editor, nice to see you this afternoon."

He picked up a brown file and unlaced the string that bound it. Inside, papers unfolded in thirds, and he smoothed them flat. He looked at

Widlund and said, "Sir, this is a meeting of the Garden County Insanity Board. It is our duty to investigate allegations of improper behavior due to insanity. Our objective under Nebraska State Law is to protect the citizens of this county and to get help for those in need. Our proceedings, sir, are conducted in closed session and are not open to the press. I must ask you to leave."

Widlund glared. "Sir, I am here on a matter that regards my sister-in-law and her husband. I believe the law allows my attendance, if Mr. and Mrs. Sutton wish it."

"We do," Sutton said.

Bronson grinned. "Of course, Mr. Widlund. This board respects the right of the defendant and the rights of the family. Mr. Buck, would you please render a ruling on the matter of Mr. Widlund's presence?"

He turned to Buck.

"Doctor Bronson, this meeting can allow only the spouse. Mr. Widlund is not permitted."

"Well, there you have it, Charles. Good day."

Widlund turned to Sutton and said quietly. "I will wait in the hall."

"You will wait outside, Mr. Widlund. On the street," Doc Bronson said.

Widlund stood and Sheriff Brier rose, too. The sheriff took his arm and ushered him into the hall. Soon the sheriff returned, shut the door and took his seat.

Bronson began with questions fired like shots from a gun.

"Maddie, where is your daughter?"

"She is with my sister, Mildred."

"Has she suffered any sickness?"

"She is fine."

"Your daughter is fine, is that correct?"

"Yes," Maddie said.

"Some say your daughter is dead."

"Dead?"

"Mr. Sutton, is your daughter dead?"

"Sir, you know damn well I lost a daughter in the storm."

"Your daughter is dead?"

"One of my daughters is dead," Sutton said.

"Your wife said your daughter is with Mrs. Widlund."

"She is. Almy is with Mrs. Widlund. Viola is dead."

"Is Viola dead, Mrs. Sutton?"

The dank basement air was suddenly heavy in Maddie's lungs. Sutton squirmed nervously. She looked into his eyes imploringly. She looked at the Doctor and remembered his office. She thought of her father in St. Louis. She thought of Farmer in the yard working by her father. She thought of the white handkerchief with red strawberries embroidered that Farmer always wore. She remembered the storm when she could not find her. She remembered the cold night, when darkness was so heavy that she wanted to cut it apart and burn it piece by piece in the fire. She remembered the morning, opening the root cellar door, pushing the snow away, going into the cold, tying the tether to the door. She remembered falling into the drifts, pulling herself up, moving left and right. She remembered the rope swishing across the top of the drifts, and she saw in her mind's eye the snag.

"NO!" she yelled. "NO! NO!"

Sutton put his arms around her, and she buried her face in his chest, sobbing loudly. He spoke softly, All right, Maddie. All right. It's OK. I'm here.

Bronson said, "Mr. Buck, what is your judgment?"

"Commission, sir."

"Mr. Deast?"

"Commission."

"Mr. Jorgensen?"

"Commission."

"The Insanity Board of Garden County, Nebraska, finds the defendant, Madelaine Sutton, insane and orders commission to the State Hospital in Hastings. Case closed. Sheriff Brier, remove the defendant immediately and see that she is locked up. Transport her to the State Hospital in Hastings as soon as the next train can carry her. Remove her! "

Sutton rushed toward Bronson and grabbed his collar. "You can't do this!" but Brier pulled him back and said, "Calm yourself, Mr. Sutton, or face arrest."

Sutton stood aside, shaking with anger. Brier took Maddie's arm, and she went sobbing out the door with him. Sutton glared at the Doctor. Deast said, "You best leave, Sutton."

Jorgensen stood at Deast's side. Bronson grinned as he adjusted his coat, then he turned and went out. Jorgensen and Deast followed.

Alone, Sutton had no answer. The afternoon sun waned, and the basement room darkened. He heard footsteps click on the floor directly above him, then a door clacked shut. He lifted his hands to his eyes and rotated them slowly. The black tips were now pinched where the undamaged flesh began, and the nails, streaked grotesquely with purple, were loose and yellow. He wondered how many days it would be before they fell away, or if he would have power and dexterity after they were gone. He pictured Bronson's pink neck and his sneering thin lips, and Maddie going quietly out the door with the sheriff's rough hand gripping her elbow. The image was vivid, and he knew it would not go away.

19

Chokecherry Valley

THE RIDE from Rackett to Oshkosh is twenty-two miles, and Rootes Jackson had covered half of them on his black mule when he stopped at the highest point of the rutted road. He dismounted, took his saddlebag from the animal and perched himself on a patch of bluestem. He looked west, across the rolling hills greening in the early spring.

He opened the saddle bag, took the canteen and drank the water from the well on his homestead. The water, warmed from the mule's flank, trickled down his throat slowly. He consumed only a little. He replaced the canteen and in the same motion removed his sketchbook and charcoal. He found a blank page and began to draw: Grass, hills, waterfowl veed against the cloudless sky. He detailed his sketch with tipis from which trails of smoke emerged hopefully. He set his imagination loose, and began to see the snow, the drifts and the starving children desperate for warmth and food. He provided for them a visible elk herd only yards away, and then made warriors to hunt them. As if the tribe were in motion, he made a returning band dragging a carcass, and children and women waiting.

He titled the picture, "Winter 1878," then sat in thought. The old Cheyenne woman was clear in his mind. He sat with her when he came to the Sand Hills country from the north, years ago.

"What once happens in a place is always happening," she told him.

Her words inspired him when he filed for his Kincaid, and they sustained him when, alone in his ambition, he considered abandoning his claim and his dream. It meant that doing right would return rightly done. He hadn't always done it; who could? She said Little Wolf didn't believe the white man. To evade the soldiers and find a winter camp, he took his people to the valley of the chokecherries. It was a valley so sheltered it was like her cupped hands, which she held trembling before him. The winter was harsh, and many died. But the soldiers did not find them.

He studied the land below but could not find what he searched for. Then his eyes paused on an unnaturally bare patch, and he saw the trail that would lead to the valley. A sacred valley to him, and he would walk there.

He returned the sketchbook and saddlebag to the back of the mule. He dropped the reins and the animal grazed tentatively, trained to wait. He picketed the animal, descended the hill until he found the trail, and headed into the valley. The early spring sun was on his back. In a half hour he had walked through a draw between two hills and into the valley.

He felt at once the presence of the people he had sketched, imagining. He stood without motion and heard the sounds of muffled groans. He heard an infant cry and saw a mother give it breast. He heard a man grunt orders. He heard a child call to a friend and then an assertive laugh which was soon answered in kind. He paused a while to absorb the sounds, and as he remained still, more ghosts emerged. The village people moved before his eyes. In their gaunt faces he saw hunger as if it were a silent old man on a cold bench. On wrists grown thin with starvation he saw tired veins, purple against deeply browned skin, and on the tips of fingers he saw rotting black flesh, the telltale mark of frostbite.

He turned after several minutes. Walking slowly and without looking back, he emerged from this sacred valley where those native to this land hid from white soldiers who pursued them and their land. He had not counted the number of people he imagined, nor did he know how many had died there. He felt their suffering, felt it in his soul, and kindred spirit of oppressed people, and whether it was one or a hundred native Americans who suffered, the importance of it was no greater nor no less to him.

He cleared the rise, crossed a shallow depression, then wended his way through a trough of sand between the hills, each arched toward the southeast. He began a slow leftward turn, and he started up to the mule maybe a hundred yards away. He froze. Silhouetted against the sky were four men. Three moved freely, but one was still. He was bound, hands behind his back. Light was behind them, and he could not recognize the faces.

He moved slowly to a crouch, and the men did not notice his motion. He crawled on his stomach to his right, away from the faint trail, and hid behind the tallest of the bluestem. With changes in the breeze, he could hear occasional pieces of the talk.

"...Jackson..."

"...you'll pay..."

He crawled closer. More information. Who? Why? Captive? In trouble? He sorted his options, planned. Moved closer. Cut the distance to twenty-five yards. There was little cover, only indentations in the sand. He could be easily spotted if the men turned. The captive might see him and could reveal him. Jackson settled deep as if he were sand.

He had no weapon. Retreating was possible, perhaps slowly and deliberately, after achieving the ridge line of the hill he had ridden up from the south. He could inch his way down into the trough, then move toward the sacred valley out of sight. That would leave the captive alone with his trouble. Maybe he could overtake them later, but surely they would take his mule and his water. He saw no choice.

He stood and with long, deliberate strides came quickly on the group.

He shouted, "Heah! Heah! What's going on?"

One said, "You black bastard, git your ass up here."

"You get away from that mule! Who sent you out here?"

The captive yelled, "It's me, Dimon. Run, Rootes! They mean trouble!"

The shortest of the group pushed the captive to the ground and delivered a back hand to his head and he slumped. The little man kicked hard, and Dimon yelped when the boot cracked his ribs.

Jackson charged the group, running. He lowered his head and bore down on the little man, who tried to dodge. Jackson veered sharply, too fast for the little man, and drove his head deep into the little man's chest. The others didn't move.

The little man tumbled backwards, grabbed his chest as he rolled on the ground, gasping for air. Jackson piled on him and found his neck with his large hands and squeezed. The others watched momentarily, then one drew his pistol and fired. Jackson did not stop, and the little man gagged and his tongue seeped from the side of his mouth. Blood sopped through the shoulder of Jackson's shirt and vest, but his grip tightened on the little man. The man with the pistol walked slowly to Jackson and put the barrel of the pistol to Jackson's head and fired.

The sound echoed through the sacred valley and across the hills and back to the ears of the slumping captive, the motionless little man, and the man with the pistol and the other who seemed to have turned to stone. Jackson's head was halved, and the brains and blood were spread across the little man, and Jackson's heavy body fell grotesquely across the legs of the little man. There was no movement in either man.

The man with the pistol said to the other, "Kill him! Kill the sonnabitch right now! Kill him!"

The other looked at the man with the pistol and then at Dimon, who lay on the ground moaning. He wore his hair long, white and curly, and it gushed from the sides of his felt hat. To Dimon he seemed to have become suddenly in charge, commanding the situation, and Dimon was relieved.

"You have the pistol. You kill 'im. Deast wants 'em both dead, like he said. Kill 'im yerself, Lonnie."

"What we gonna do with the bodies, for god's sake? What we gonna do?" the man called Lonnie said. "What we gonna do with that mule?"

The other man said nothing. He waited, but Lonnie stood quietly and did not move. He went to Dimon and looked down on him. He stooped, and when he did his hat fell, and Dimon could see the locks of white curls spilling from his head. The white-haired man took Dimon under the shoulders and lifted him to his feet, but Dimon had too much pain in his ribs and slumped again to the ground.

The white-haired man said, "Lonnie, you pull your little dead friend away from this place. Pull him down to that low place, and scoop out a sand grave as deep as you can. You put him there."

"The hell!" "I ain't gonna do that, Frosty!" Lonnie yelped.

"Shut it! Do it!" the white-haired man said.

Lonnie obeyed. He took the little man by his arms and dragged him down the hill and found a low place. With his bare hands he began to dig a shallow grave.

The white-haired man took a rope from his saddle and tied it around Jackson's two legs. He mounted his horse and wrapped the rope around the saddle horn. He spurred the animal and the rope snugged taut. With another spur, the animal moved Jackson's corpse down the hill in the other direction. When he had pulled Jackson's body several yards, the white-haired man discovered the faint trail and began to follow it with Jackson's body dragging over the bluestem and through the sand. The horse resisted, so he spurred him on.

Then he sat his horse and looked back to the top of the hill. Only the captive and the mule were visible. Lonnie was not in sight, and his horse was gone.

The white-haired man reined his horse and followed the trail the same way Jackson had earlier gone. When he thought he had gone far enough off the rutted road, he halted his horse and reined it backward. The rope loosened, and he dismounted. He removed the rope from Jackson's legs and coiled it calmly. He saw the footprints where Jackson had earlier stood, and he could tell that Jackson had roamed some in this spot before turning back. The tracks told him Jackson had gone no further, and he decided he was far enough away from the rutted road.

With his hands he began to dig, and for once he was glad this land was made mostly of sand. He found a stone, and with it carved the grave deeper. When he had brought it low enough, he rolled Jackson's body into it, then turned the dead man until his face was up but the features from the black ears forward were clotting blood, the rest blown away. Then he pushed sand over the body. When it was covered and mounded, he mounted his horse and reined it over the grave, back and forth. The hooves pushed deep into the sand and the mound settled.

The white-haired man rode out the same way. He found Dimon on top of the hill, his hands still tied behind his back. He dismounted, and with his knife cut the rope.

"You're gonna make it. Your ribs gonna hurt like hell for a while. You think you can get that black mule home?"

The captive studied his captor's face. The other man's eyes were blue, almost clear, his face shaved and his jaw square.

Dimon said, "Why are you letting me go?"

"This business here is no damn good."

Dimon stood, but when he tried to mount the mule, the pain pushed him back. The white-haired man stooped to take the captive's boot heel and fitted it into the stirrup. Then he laced his fingers and nodded for the captive to use them. The black mule stood perfectly still, as if it understood. When the captive was mounted, he took the reins, slumping forward to ease the pain in his ribs. He offered to shake the hand of the white-haired man, and the man only nodded.

"Git on, now," he said.

When he had ridden several minutes, Dimon looked back, toward the valley where his friend, the loyal Rootes Jackson, lay buried. The white-haired man whose name was Frosty was not there.

20

The Special Agent

SPECIAL AGENT Rodney Ruhoff sat at a small table in his hotel room in Rackett and wrote a note to his wife back home in Washington. It was his first month in western Nebraska, and it turned out to be about as he expected. That is, except for the illegal fencing he was assigned to investigate. It was far more extensive than he thought.

He hoped to get home by mid-summer, but here in early May, he was thinking he'd be lucky to make it by Christmas. What was shaping up, in Ruhoff's view, was a showdown between U.S. Attorney Irving W. Baxter and the cattlemen. The case his boss thought would be pivotal was dependent on what Ruhoff could dig up concerning a western Nebraska cattleman named Rutherford Gaines Deast, the principal owner of Deast Land and Cattle Co.

What Ruhoff had discovered so far involved two widows, one in Grand Island and the other in Omaha. Both told Ruhoff they would testify that they were approached by a man named Buckner Larson, who offered each widow a hundred dollars to file a claim in the Sand Hills under the new Kincaid Act. Larson was an Omaha attorney who had Deast as his client. He intended to use the widows to make claims they couldn't support then ,on Deast's behalf, he could grab the claims for his client, alleging they had been abandoned. He told the widows western Nebraska was being settled quickly because of this new law, and they could take advantage of a clause that allowed them to make a claim without having to live there. Both were eager to get in on the deal.

One was named Meredith A. Tomppert and the other was Catherine Garland Reeser. The story was easily believed by the unsuspecting widows, and Larson came away with the signed papers he would need to make the two fraudulent entries near Rackett.

When Ruhoff learned the approximate location of these entries, he discovered they included federal land that was illegally fenced. What's more, they partially bordered Deast ranchland, and so he suspected it was Deast's operation that was responsible for illegally enclosing federal land. The evidence of land fraud was what Ruhoff and his boss were looking for, and the case was strengthening, but now he suspected illegal enclosures as well.

But the story told by a settler south toward Oshkosh was even more alarming. This man, David Dimon, accused Deast and several of his men of intimidation, death threats, property destruction, even assault.

He finished his letter, then went down the wooden stairs to the ornate lobby of the nearly new Rackett Hotel. Beneath an ostentatious chandelier suspended from plastered quatrefoil sat an elegant man in a winged back chair. A golden chain dipped twice before one end disappeared in a watch pocket. When the man saw Ruhoff, he extracted the watch, looked long at it, and then replaced it precisely. He lifted his eyes slowly and Ruhoff noticeably cringed when he slowly said, "Good morning, Mr. Ruhoff."

"Good morning to you, sir," he said. The man rose gracefully, and with a nearly imperceptible bow motioned Ruhoff toward the hotel dining room.

They found their table, and Elias Hunter unfolded his napkin and with a sweeping gesture and settled it on his lap. He adjusted his pince nez and then placed both hands on the table, where they rested patiently, like fat mice in a feed store. The waiter arrived and they ordered, toast and coffee for Hunter and steak and eggs for Ruhoff.

"What have you learned?" Hunter asked.

Ruhoff spoke quickly in soft tones as he outlined what he knew about the widow entries. With the help of a locater named Coulson as a guide, he had ridden to the claims and substantiated that federal land was illegally enclosed. What's more, Coulson had told him of intimidation and threats made by the cattleman. Coulson, Ruhoff told Hunter, was a highly respected, no- nonsense person who would make an excellent witness. Dimon, older and frenetic, was supported in his claim by Coulson. And there was another potential witness, a black man named Rootes Jackson.

"A black man?" Hunter asked.

"Proved-up near Oshkosh. Tough as nails, reputed to be."

"You've talked to Coulson and this Jackson?"

"Just Coulson. Jackson comes here occasionally."

"We need him."

Hunter is as upright as a statue, Ruhoff thought. Stiff and proper. Washington, not country. He watched Hunter lift his coffee delicately and purse his lips for a small sip. He pinched the cup handle between his thumb and index finger, his pinkie cocked stiff like the tail of a prairie chicken.

"I have interviewed with the newspaper," Hunter said after a pause. "The *Tribune* will inform the people of our intentions. There will be law. Only the illegal operators have anything to worry about. Honest cattlemen have no worry."

Ruhoff let the announcement float away, adding nothing. He held his eyes on Hunter's face and studied his affected motions. Ruhoff thought Hunter's mannerisms betrayed a man who isn't sure of himself and who compensates with practiced movements and expressions. He let the idea lie; regardless, Hunter was the boss.

"I informed the editor that government agents are in the territory, assigned by the top attorney in the land to investigate the fencing situation. I told him that every fence in this section of the country must come off government land. There will be no delays, and immediate prosecution of all offenders would be carried forward, regardless of expense."

Facing the window, Hunter seemed illuminated. The mid- morning sunlight streamed through the windows, and the white tablecloth glowed. His slickened black hair gleamed, emphasizing the symmetrical waves of it lifting from the parted center.

"Mr. Baxter wants this, Rodney. He is under pressure from the president. An example must be made of Deast. Others doing the same thing will hear of it. Respect for the law will change their behavior."

Ruhoff chewed quietly. U.S. Attorney Baxter certainly would not want to cross the president, but he doubted he'd offend the wealthiest people in western Nebraska any more than he had to.

"There is sympathy for the cattlemen here. Money works for them. Sodders have nothing. Do you expect the general public to support the cases we bring?"

"I believe the newspaper man agrees, generally. In any event, it's not the people's say, Rodney. The law has been written. We will bring the case. Judge Munger is said to be fair. What the cattlemen bully away will be returned. They cannot be allowed to prevail against the power of law."

"I think we are close with Deast. What else should we get?"

"You should get the black man in the fold. You talk to him, and we can follow up with a deposition."

"His testimony will support the old man's."

Daubing at his lips with his napkin, Hunter said, "Get him on record."

21

Sutton returns

EVEN BUTTONING his pants was a chore. The wasting tips of his frostbitten fingers were not painful, but the absence of dexterity made him long for the rotting process to be over. He stood at the workbench by the open passageway and held the hatchet with his dominant right hand. He made the mock motion of lifting the implement then bringing it down hard on the tips. Then he rehearsed the action with the hatchet in his left hand, and it was clear there would be no precision. Missing the target could mean a far more painful amputation and a much longer recovery time. There was work to do, and he did not want to involve any more of his time with his rotting fingers.

He stepped under the lintel that held the barn entryway open. Someday he'd put a door on the barn, but for now the animals had protection enough from the northwest winds. He paused to admire his pronghorn trophy and vowed again to straighten it. He went into the yard, heard a holler.

"Ho! Sutton!"

He looked up the road and saw Dimon coming at a trot. The old man dismounted and rushed to him, waving his arms.

"There's news, Will!"

"What?"

"Thought I'd met the end!"

"What!?"

"Deast's men came into my place and hauled me away!"

"The hell! What are you talking about?"

"Rootes Jackson is dead! They spared me, but, damn, Sutton, I'm lucky to be alive!"

Dimon spilled the rest of the story in blurted exclamations, and Sutton tried his best to decipher it. Dimon said he'd never seen the men; they weren't the ones who were on his land before. They were Deast's men; he was sure of it.

The captors said they wanted Jackson, and Dimon told them where to look, thinking they'd leave him. But they took him with them, tied with rope, and walked him alongside their horses. They headed south toward the Jackson homestead and happened upon Jackson's mule in the hills. Pure accident they found him, Dimon said. Jackson rushed 'em and damn near disarmed the whole gang, but they shot him, he said.

"You saw 'em kill Jackson?"

"Goddamn, Sutton! Put a revolver to his head!"

"Where?"

"South, halfway. The vista point up there."

Dimon said one of them showed him mercy and untied him and sent him off on Jackson's mule.

"Why'd he do that?"

"I don't know, Sutton. I sure as hell don't know. He took Jackson's body away, too. Must have buried it. Rootes got one of 'em. Goddamn, Sutton, the man was the bravest I ever seen. He got the little bastard's throat and squeezed the life out of him."

"Jesus!" Sutton said.

"The shorty one's buried out there, too. I know it. One of 'em rode away, and the Mercy Man -- hell, I don't know where he go'ed."

Dimon ranted on. Sutton turned away with no answer, trying to make sense of his story. Dimon was witness to a murder and victim of kidnapping. If Deast was behind it, there was more than illegal fencing on his hands. There was blood.

"What we gonna do, Sutton? These boys gotta be stopped."

"Dimon, these fingers need tending to. You go on home. Keep your gun loaded. Jesus!"

* * *

Sutton paused at the open south door of the hut and looked for a moment on his daughter as she swept the floor. Her hair tangled in russet tones and bunched in curls, she looked womanly. For a moment it wasn't Almy he saw; it was Maddie returned to the homestead and happily at work again. He remembered his wife's voice humming softly. Then he was again in the courthouse, seeing her confused face as the men before her committed her to the asylum, and the sinister sneer of the doctor was before him in hues clarified by time and hurt. They had ushered her out, and she had said nothing, and when he went to look, he could not find her. They had held her in jail until the night train stopped, then sent a deputy with her to the Hastings asylum.

"Pa ...?"

"Ah ... yes. Some tea?"

"Water's on, Pa. You sit there and I'll fix it."

He sat on the bench and removed his hat. Almy brought the cup and placed it in front of him. He put his arm around her waist and brought her near and she smiled into his face, level with hers.

"What'd you do with Farmer's bandana?"

Almy withdrew at the question. She dropped her head and said,

"I put it away, Pa. Didn't feel I should wear it. Belonged to Farmer, not me."

"Well, that's fine. You keep it safe; I know you will."

Quietly, they sat with tea.

"What did Mr. Dimon want?"

Sutton blurted, "I'm going to Rackett tomorrow. I'm saddling up the mare and I'm going to town, and I will be gone three nights. You are to stay here and tend to chores. You will be fine."

She went to the stove and pushed the kettle to the back. She opened the burner cover, smoothed the coals and replaced the lid, as if she'd done it a thousand times. She took the cast-iron pot from the shelf and placed in on the front. Catching glances at Sutton while she worked, she put in the chicken carcass along with a chopped garden onion from the cellar and new-growth arrowhead tubers she harvested from the pond, and filled the pot with water. She stirred the contents slowly, and the aroma filled the hut.

"I will be fine, Pa. Why do you go?"

"Uncle Charles is right. I need to do something with these fingers. Too much work to do. I'll have Doc fix 'em then get back here for chores."

Her thoughts blurred. Doc. The fingers. Her uncle and aunt. The town. The bandana.

She said, "Is Mr. Dimon OK?"

"Yep. Things are fine."

She stirred the broth and arranged utensils on the counter. "I'd like to go."

"It's better you stay and tend to chores here. That will be it. I leave before dawn."

The girl turned to the broth she was making and stirred it before replacing the cast iron lid. She did not want to be alone in the hut.

* * *

Alone on horseback, the ride went quickly. Sutton stayed the night with the Widlunds. Over coffee the next morning, he told Charles his intention. Both sat in long silence. Widlund wasn't sure. Sutton should get the fingers fixed and get on with the healing. Doc's amputation would be better than the long wait for nature to take its course, but the thought of Doc caused a grind in his stomach. He looked long at Sutton's face and knew his brother-in-law's hurt was even deeper and his hate even sharper. He didn't know how Sutton could face the man.

"You want me or Mildred there?"

"No."

"Doc's a cheat," Widlund said. "Maddie was doing better. They want your claim, Will. Doc's as much a part of it as Deast."

Sutton brought his eyes to Widlund's face. A mix of images drifted between their locked gaze, as if they both were seeing the past and the future all come together. The *Tribune* was lying on the table, and Widlund picked it up.

"Federal agents from Interior are here, Will. I talked with the supervisor. They say they mean business with the illegal enclosures. Story in this week's edition."

He pushed the paper at Sutton, who glossed the article, put the paper down and thought, his eyes glancing toward Widlund.

"There's more than fencing, Charles."

"What?"

"Deast boys making a lot of trouble. Dimon was threatened. I don't know if he's lost his marbles or what. He says there was a killing."

"Dimon says somebody got killed? Over what, for heaven's sake?"

"Same as usual. Homesteaders beating 'em to the patents on government land. They aim to keep their cattle grazing inside the fences they put up, legal or not."

"Law is in the 'steaders' favor, Will."

"You argue it in the paper, Charles. Most of the folks around here not eager to pick a fight with the big cattle boys, and you ought to remember it. If Dimon ain't crazy, there are a couple of dead men out there in the hills south of us. Don't need no more killin'. Sure as hell don't need your veins pouring blood into the streets of Rackett."

"You know the dead man?"

"Nope. Friend of Dimon's from near Oshkosh. Says he's a black man named Jackson."

"Sheriff know?"

"Or care? Hell, nobody knows 'cept Dimon, and he might be hearing voices for all I know. Dimon swears it though. Says Deast's men hauled him away and all of 'em went lookin' for Jackson. Ruckus ensued and two men died, one of the men Dimon says was on Deast's errand and the other a proved-up settler. Dimon said he was shot point blank in the head."

Widlund picked up his paper.

"Listen, Will. Listen what they told me.

"Says here, 'The *Tribune* has interviewed Mr. Elias Hunter, director of special agents of the General Land Office, who had been sent to Rackett from Washington to investigate the fencing situation. Mr. Hunter stated flatly that every fence in this section of the country must come off government land. He said no more delays or intermissions will be granted and the immediate prosecution of all offenders will be carried forward regardless of expense. Mr. Hunter discussed the current cases the government has in process and said these are only the beginning, as the government intends to force everyone to obey the law and thereby give all persons equal access to public land.' "

Widlund put the paper down and sipped his coffee. Sutton said, "Yep; I see it, Charles. Well, I guess everybody in Garden County has their ears up on that one. At least the ones that read that damned paper of yours."

"There's something else, Will. You ever hear of a woman settler named Tomppert? Made entry on a section up by you somewhere?"

"Never heard the name, no." "Well, she's about to prove up."

Sutton leaned back in his chair and raised his hands slowly, turning the black tips front and back. The pinch was deeper where the dead flesh stopped and the live flesh began. Cut off or sloughed off, the rotten flesh would soon enough be gone, and he'd be left with stubs to remind him. He wondered how he'd do, what compensations he'd make. In the end, it wasn't so different than anything else. Figure it out and get on with it.

"From her rocking chair in Omaha, I suspect," Sutton said.

"Rocking and counting the dollar bills somebody paid her," Widlund added.

22

Widlund and Bronson talk

"DOCTORING'S MY skill, not precisely my interest," Doc Bronson offered.

Widlund reclined in his creaky desk chair. He studied Bronson's smile, which seemed to respond to an unspoken irony. It was unusual for Doc to stop by to chat. To Widlund, Doc always remained aloof. The two men weren't rivals, but neither were they friends. They seemed to have respected a line drawn between them. Widlund had never known Doc to talk about himself. Now the man was casually open, curiously eager to talk.

Widlund noticed that Bronson's blue eyes, facing the gooseneck lamp on Widlund's desk, sparked with smugness, some unspoken inward satisfaction. His unnaturally white teeth suggested self- indulgence, as if he had just picked and then polished them. Widlund found the face unnerving, as if unstable chemicals swirled beneath the skin. He couldn't be sure if the man was handsome; that idea seemed irresoluble, but he wondered if women found the doctor attractive.

"Not very comforting, Doctor, for the sick and injured of the county."

"They get what they need."

Widlund peered through the smoky window above the Linotype as if seeking an escape. Bronson's chatter was a distraction.

"And tell me, Mr. Editor, what brought you here. Some higher cause?"

"There's no cause, Doctor. Just work, meaningful work."

"Ah, 'meaningful.' Work that brings riches then? Work that brings adventure? Or just work? For me, Mr. Editor, adventure is the higher cause; riches nip at its heel."

"I would think the oath would be a guide for a physician. 'Do no harm' ..."

"Certainly. Oh! And 'issue no pessary.' And, my personal favorite, Widlund -- keeping oneself from all the pleasures of love with patients. I have found that one most useful," he said.

Widlund almost smiled but reconsidered. He was not sure he wanted to be part of Bronson's humor. It had begun to feel like a game of verbal chess, something said with the intention of causing a particular effect. Bronson rambled on.

"Ancient morals -- vapid in today's modern world, Widlund. Medicine requires them, I suppose, to assure the commoners among us, if not merely to give high-mindedness an oppressor. I choose to augment my life with other adventures."

The tease caught him, and Widlund asked for detail.

"Trails. I enjoy following the trails."

"What trails?"

Arrogance was nothing new for Doc, Widlund thought, but he had not seen him reckless. Encouraged, Bronson leaned back and folded his arms across his hollow chest. He extended his legs so far that he appeared reclined like a Roman at dinner. He ran his fingers through his sandy hair once and then again, examining the palm of his hand as if it had sifted gold.

"Let me give you an example of how choices present themselves, and decisions determine direction. My home was in Boston, and my upbringing proper Christian. My family were members of the finest Baptist faith. All the trappings of a Brahmin life lay ahead. Education, at which I excelled. Comfort, of which my family had plenty. Literature and elevated conversation with writers and physicians -- all were mine by birth."

Widlund shifted his weight. He tightened his jaw to hide the disdain he wanted to display for the small man. He trained himself to be fair-minded, and his challenge sat across from him.

"By my sixteenth year, a course had been set. What decision I may have made I cannot say, except for behavior. My own pastor declared me unfit -- 'Worse than the Devil!' he announced -- and I was expelled. This is the trail to which I refer; the trail of adventure that led me here to this virgin country is a deliberate turn from the trail of Boston gentility. Here I invest in cattle, land and doctoring, and the biggest lure of all -- adventure!"

"Expelled? A trail of adventure? My, my doctor. I don't mean to be rude, but to me these suggest an inauspicious beginning. You remain unchurched then?"

"A baby begins with severed umbilical cord and grows to manhood. So, the cut from the tyranny of the Baptist church was for me the beginning of an adventurous life. Morals must be framed by situation, don't you agree? Especially here on the prairie."

Widlund stood abruptly. He went for the pot of coffee, vile with black stain, simmering on the woodstove, then poured cups for both of them.

"The ethics you outline do not fit my understanding of civilized life, Doctor."

"We are growing our civilization. A blank slate. Absolutes are a waste of time. Who among us isn't pragmatic?"

"Blank? This country has been settled for thirty years now, Doc. It's not blank."

"The ink is still wet, isn't it, Mr. Editor. Even your ink. Let me show you."

He rose and went to the door.

"Come."

Widlund put his cup down and went with Bronson, who led him next door to his office. He unlocked the door and led Widlund to the examination room, and he stood beside his bookcase.

"A gift of Glanton," he said.

He held the scalp box proudly, and Widlund looked inside hoping to see something new. He'd seen the doctor do this before, and this time bravado blended with the bragging way the man had just explained his history. He knew what the doctor would say, and he did.

"The trophy was taken in the Mexican territory forty years ago. It belonged on the head of an Apache, scalped clean for fifty dollars' bounty. You see, Widlund, the ink is not yet dry."

Widlund looked at the bookshelf. Other trophies had been placed there, arrowheads, arrows, a bow. The skull of a rabbit. A human skull. And Farmer's bandana.

"What is this?"

Widlund took the handkerchief and turned in slowly in his hand. The red strawberries seemed pale against the unwashed white cloth. The splotches of blood had dried and were nearly black, and Widlund knew.

"This belongs to my niece. Why do you have it?"

"Ah. She must have dropped it when she was here for her fever, Mr. Editor."

"And the blood?"

"Blood? Well, I don't know. Perhaps a cut on her hand," he said.

Widlund without invitation sat in the doctor's chair. He leaned back calmly and studied the doctor who stood before him, as if the doctor were the patient. He took in the whole man, the hair, the blue eyes, the shortness in stature, the ill-defined smile, the sandy hair.

"Doc, Mrs. Sutton is not insane."

"Of course she is. I know she's your sister-in-law, but the woman is crazy, Widlund. A threat to our society. The Insanity Board is quite correct to commit her."

"You and the cattleman want the homestead. You want her out of the way. You want Sutton to give it up. Is that what you're conspiring?"

"You think too little of me, Widlund."

"And this handkerchief. I will ask Almy about the sequence of events, Doc. I will be interested to hear her version of the story. Did you ask her for it? Is it another of your trophies?"

Doc moved toward Widlund who sat up defensively. Doc bent at the waist and put his head near Widlund's. He raised his chin and spoke through his teeth, as if holding back a floodgate of anger.

"You had best think what you're suggesting, sir."

Widlund put his hand on the man's shoulder and pushed him away. He rose from the chair and stepped toward the door. He turned to go, but paused and then returned to the doctor, and faced him squarely.

"I will give it lots of thought, Bronson. Lots of thought."

23

The choice

MILDRED covered her table with white linen and arranged a deep blue brocade runner decorated with a tatting of gold thread. She placed armed chairs around the oval table with great care, assuring symmetry and balance, and if arbitrarily disturbed, she would re-position them without thinking. At the center of the table she placed a silver tray, and at its center were creamer and salt and pepper shakers. Two silver candle holders, with lighted tapers, guarded the outer flanks like statuesque sentries.

Her fine memory, as organized as her dining room, kept track of the many conversations over dinner. She wove the threads of thought creatively, as if each had a place in her own intellectual tapestry. As conversation sharpened, she would sit quietly at the foot of the table in the position closest to her kitchen. She

weighed the pieces of conversation carefully, and she spoke little and smiled often, her inquisitive eyes clear with understanding. At times when her guests' plates needed attention, she would seem to float to the proper shoulder to serve or to clear as if an apparition.

Her meals were carefully prepared from the best available products in season. She relished the process, as an artist might anticipate the moments in studio with easel and palette. From practice and attention, she knew the duration of nearly every course, and she could easily anticipate which serving would be followed by the cleverest ideas. Food, she knew, nurtured more than body and limb; it was energy for conversation.

At this table Sutton sat with his hands folded and the blackened finger tips exposed. He sat upright, and forgetting, rested his elbows on the table.

Mildred moved to his left and offered a serving of potatoes followed by gravy. He accepted with a kindly nod, catching her eyes in a moment that each knew was acknowledgement of their mutual loss. Her sister had chosen wisely, she knew, and Sutton, with no real ability to say so, appreciated his in-laws.

Widlund adjusted his cloth napkin with little notice. His thoughts were on the confrontation that morning. He weighed the choices before him. What outcome? What reaction? What consequence?

When Mildred served the beef for Sutton, then carved it as a mother would for a toddler, he decided.

"When do you plan to see the doctor, Will?" "Tomorrow."

"You've talked with him?" "No."

Widlund chewed. When he swallowed, he wiped his lips and mustache with the linen napkin.

"He wants your claim, Will." "I know that."

"He has taken Maddie away because he's in cahoots with the cattleman."

"I know that."

"Yet you plan to let him amputate those fingers?" "I do. Tomorrow."

Widlund was quiet for the moment it took to consider his options. He decided to tell what he saw.

"Bronson has Farmer's bandana."

Sutton was caught mid-swallow. Almy had lied? Not put it in safekeeping? Widlund went on.

"He has it in his examination room. With other keepsakes of his. I do not like what it suggests. We do not know the full story. Almy can tell us. We should ask her to tell us."

"She is alone at the hut."

"Of course. You will have to wait. See the doctor later."

"Maybe, Charles. You saw the bandana there? What did he say about it?"

"He was angry when I asked him about it. I don't trust him."

"He's the only doc we have. I'm no good without my hands, Charles. I need to be done with this storm and these fingers it left me with. I have work to do. And I need Maddie."

At the mention of her sister's name, Mildred wondered how her sister was doing. She imagined squalid conditions at the asylum, but she didn't know anything for sure. She hoped she was under good care, but there was no information. Maddie had not written.

"Maddie was making progress before this ridiculous Insanity Board got involved," she said. "Their concern for the community! I doubt it. I think we should make an appeal to the head of the hospital in Hastings, Will. Charles, will you help write a letter? This should be appealed. The experience was horrible for her, and her breakdown was temporary. She needs to come home."

Widlund said, "I will certainly help write a letter. We will describe exactly what has happened, and we will fully disclose the trickery and the haste with which she was dispatched to the asylum. It might be that the officials there will conduct their own assessment of her condition."

Sutton was not eating. He examined his fingers. The nails turned yellower darker. The dead flesh held loosely to the first knuckles. The healing from amputation would be quick, thorough. The stubs would suffice in the field and on the plow and with the horses. Almy needed the support; she shouldered too much alone, just a child weighted with heartbreak.

"I will see him tomorrow. I've been thinking more and more of it. I have decided to move ahead with this, Charles."

"I'll go with you."

"No, Charles. I will be fine, and tomorrow with my hand bandaged, I will return to the soddie and complete my own doctoring. This won't take long, and it will be good."

Mildred rose and began to clear. She placed the dishes in her kitchen and returned with a cake she had made from cellared carrots. Sutton declined, rising from the table and bowing slightly.

He and Widlund moved to the drawing room and sat momentarily. Then he rose, said his thank-yous and properly thanked Mildred. Then he went to the room he and Maddie always shared when they visited. He quickly fell asleep.

<u>24</u>

The invitation

THE NEXT morning, Sutton dressed himself and gathered his things. He went directly to the doctor's office and walked in. There were no patients in the waiting room. The door to Bronson's office was partially open, and he pushed it with a bang and entered.

Bronson was not in the room. Sutton went to the shelves behind Bronson's desk, and he sorted through the keepsakes. He picked up the box with the scalp inside. He placed it on the desk and then examined the shelves. He saw the Indian relics, and Bronson's books with titles he didn't recognize. He saw books on medicine and anatomy, bookmarked at places the doctor often used. He started at the top of the bookshelves and worked his eyes down, but there was no bandana belonging to Almy. He thought he must have overlooked it, so he repeated the process. Nothing.

The doctor entered through the back door suddenly. He saw Bronson in his office. The two men eyed each other, and no words were spoken until the doctor, moving sideways around the edge of the room, found his place behind the desk.

"You came to see me?"

Sutton's face relaxed, and he could see the doctor's tighten. He did not move. Sutton peered through the doctor's blue eyes, as if he were looking through a streaked window. He studied the man's face and its features.

He said, "Maddie is not insane."

"Now, Mr. Sutton, I understand your concern. We have the community to look out for, so we must take extra precautions in these cases. She is now safe."

"You have my daughter's bandana. I want you to return it now."

"Bandana?"

"You know what I'm talking about, Bronson. The bandana."

Bronson reached into his breast pocket and removed the bandana. The strawberries were brilliant red in the sun. When he saw the blackened spots were blood remained, Sutton wondered what had happened.

"I'll have that now," Sutton said.

Bronson hesitated, looked to his right and to his left in indecision. Then he offered the kerchief hesitantly, as if it were incriminating. Sutton took it without removing his eyes from Bronson's face. Then, as the doctor watched, he examined the bandana closely. He smelled it and caught the odor of Bronson's disgusting cologne.

"What is the source of these bloodstains?"

"Ah ... um, well now ... You know? Ah . . . "

Sutton put the bandana in his pocket. He went behind the doctor's desk and stopped when his boot toe stepped on Bronson's boot. His large nose was inches from Bronson. He said nothing.

Then he backed up and said without emotion,

"I want you to remove these frostbit fingers. I do not want you to do it here. I want you at the soddie so I can be with my daughter so she can dress the wounds and help me heal. Do you understand?"

"Well, Mr. Sutton, now I can't come out there. It's best we do that here."

"No. At my place. Day after tomorrow. You bring the tools you need. You will do this operation at my soddie. Do you understand?"

The doctor said, "I will bring an assistant."

"No, you will come alone. Day after tomorrow. If you need assistance, Almy will help. She is very strong. The sight of blood does not affect her. You will come."

"And if I don't . . . ?"

"My brother-in-law, perhaps you know the newspaperman. Of course, you do; you threw him out of the hearing. You talked to him yesterday. He will want to write about your failure to come to my soddie and to help me through this difficult time. The people of this territory will know about it. It will be best for you that we handle this in a way that is best for my daughter and me."

The doctor said he would come.

Sutton said, "Thank you, Doctor. I do appreciate your understanding."

"Of course, Sutton. Of course."

25

Conversation by the pond

EVENING SETTLED over Sutton Pond with the softness of cotton. A noisy band of yellow-headed blackbirds flitted among the cattails. A trio of white pelicans sailed overhead then settled on the still pond and calmed like frigates in irons. A nighthawk silhouetted against the yellow western sky, rose effortlessly, then dove straight down, its mouth spread wide like a whale feeding on krill. Sutton felt the air and heard the swishy flutter when the nighthawk turned skyward again just inches above his head. It joined with another, and the two repeated their sweep of the bug-filled air. The white bars at the edges of the long, pointed wings helped Sutton's eye follow the looping birds. When he lost sight of them, he turned his ear skyward and before long heard their 'pe-ent' call, followed by repeated dives. Almy walked with her father along a sandy trail indistinctively winding through the bench grass. She stepped lightly, as if she had no care in the world. She flushed an avocet, and it fluttered noisily away, its upward turned bill out of place at the end of the graceful russet neck and head.

Sutton marveled at his daughter's resiliency. He felt his loss; it was always with him, and he knew with certainty that hers was no less. Now they had only each other, a self-doubting man who questioned the choice to bring his family to this hardship, and a malleable little girl on the cusp of womanhood, saddled with responsibility and pierced with sadness and confusion.

His own anger was dormant. He had come quickly back to the soddie and hoped only to find some comfort there. He slept uneasily, his mind working in the dark night. When he rose, his mind tuned sharply to the work around the homestead. Then the end of the day came tenderly, a palpable moment that caught him off guard, and he thought of Maddie.

"Let's go out, Almy."

They went to the far side of the pond and moved the cattails aside as they pushed to the water's edge. As they did, a fox regarded them for a moment and then re-focused on a mouse hidden in the grass. Sutton reached for Almy's shoulder to halt her, and together they watched the hunt just a few yards away. The fox continued its hunt as if they weren't there. It circled. When the opportunity came, it leapt high, arched its lithe back, and fell snout first into the grass. When it came away with the mouse flailing in its jaws, the coyote regarded the humans proudly and walked off.

They returned to the pond's edge nearest the hut, and on a mound of sand sat quietly with their shoulders touching.

"Pa," the girl said, "I miss Farmer."

The simple declaration unleashed his pool of emotions. Tears gushed from his eyes and onto his dark cheekbones. He quickly turned his head away and hoped she did not see. With the back of his ragged sleeve, he wiped them away, his breath held in to avoid the choppy exhale that would reveal his grief. She leaned her head against his arm, concerned that she had entered the adult part of her father's world, where children aren't allowed because it is imprecise. She said nothing more. She could feel the choked breathing from within her father's chest.

They sat this way as the sky greyed. When two pintails splashed to the pond, Sutton looked up. Another pair appeared and then more. When he regained control of his breathing and could speak, he looked at his daughter.

"I have her bandana," he said.

Almy startled noticeably. She skipped her eyes from the shore to the horizon to her father's lean face and quickly downward in self-reproach.

"I am very happy to have it home, where it belongs. The doctor gave it to me," he said.

Almy looked into his eyes, wondering what he knew. He put his arm around the child and drew her near, his chin resting on her brown hair. He held her this way for moments as a chill rose from the sand.

"He asked me for it, Pa. It seemed to upset Ma so. . . "

"Was the doctor hurtful to you, child?"

"He said he wanted to cool me because I was too hot."

He did not want to inquire further. He did not want to know. But he couldn't let it be. Too many invasions by the doctor: Maddie and now Almy. He needed to know.

"Did you bleed on Farmer's bandana?"

The question paralyzed her. She did not know how to answer. She already had lied about the handkerchief and had been discovered. Could she lie to her father again? But it was not something she wanted to discuss with her father. She wanted her mothernto hold her, but she was gone, too.

Sutton tried again, feeling the child's anxiety.

"There is blood, Almy. I thought maybe you had cut yourself. Now I worry that the Doc may have hurt you. Can you tell me?"

She could not understand why she felt shame. It was a doctor.

"If the doctor is the one who made you bleed, then you can tell me, child."

She was back in the doctor's office, standing naked in front of him, and she saw the red trail down her leg, and she remembered the doctor stooping to daub it away. She remembered him rising again to his feet and then looking at her as she trembled in front of him, and she remembered his piercing eyes, and she remembered the smile that didn't mean friendliness. She thought of her mother, and Farmer's barely visible hand as her mother swatted at it with the broom. She wanted to run, and she rose and started.

Sutton gripped her tiny wrist and held it. She tugged to leave, but her father held. As night settled around them, she fell to her knees and wept loudly. She cried hard and so long. Before they rose to return to the hut it was very dark, and the waterfowl, the nighthawks and the yellow-heads had somewhere crouched in silence.

26

The gift of the Borgias

HOUSE CALLS on the prairie were not something Doc Bronson enjoyed. When he left Rackett and went into the wild land, he preferred adventure, not work. Still, Bronson had it figured how to handle Sutton. He rode the high trail out, caring little for the scenery. His objective was to get there, amputate, suture the stubs, and instruct the girl how to nurse Sutton back to health, including the pea-sized pills she was to mix with his food, three times a day.

He was absorbed in his plan when a rider on a black mule approached. He was surprised to see the neighbor Dimon. He pulled his horse up when the two intersected, Dimon said nothing.

"Mornin," Bronson said.

Dimon stared at the doctor.

Bronson said, "Something troublin' you, sir?"

"You are. Yer in with that cattleman."

"I wonder what brings you to greet a friend in such a rude manner."

"Yer no friend. Anybody in with Deast is no friend a mine."

Bronson said, "Your difference with Mr. Deast is no concern of mine. I'll bid you a good day, sir."

He spurred his horse ahead, but Dimon yelled after him.

"Them federal agents in town gonna hear everything I have to say. Ain't nobody pushin' David Dimon off'n his entry. These here hills have ears, mister."

When he heard it, Bronson turned his horse and rode straight up to Dimon.

"I am quite aware that you've been told what can happen if you make your case in federal court, sir. You'd best think again about what you want the federal agents to hear. You don't think for a minute, do you, that those federal boys are gonna listen to you?"

"And I 'spect that's another of yer threats. Well, you tell your friend Deast it ain't gonna go well for him in federal court."

Dimon kicked the old mule ahead. Bronson sat his horse and watched. The old man had seen too much, including what happened with the black man. He talked too much. Deast's men should have ended him. Meantime, he focused on the other entry they needed, and that's where his business took him this morning. As he rode, he reached in the bag tethered to the saddle horn. He opened it and removed the bottle. The label said, "Arsenic." Inside were several pills about the size of a small pea. Sutton's fingers needed a doctor all right, but his pain would soon go away and so would one obstacle to Deast's cattle kingdom in which Bronson had majority interest.

27

The amputation

HE TURNED the horse into Sutton's lane and saw the man waiting by the barn. He looked for the girl but couldn't see any sign of her. He reined the horse in and dismounted. Sutton had not moved.

"We'll do this in the barn," Sutton said. But first I have a question for ya, Doc."

Bronson squared against the antagonistic man who stood before him, taut like the wire on a fence.

"I can tell you what you'll need to know about these fingers, Will."

Sutton lifted both hands and held them palms up. The Doc stepped closer and lightly held the man's wrist, turning the hands slowly. The tip of each finger had turned black. The nails were the color of a cattail shaft, a lifeless purpole toward the ragged edges. Where the blood continued to flow, the flesh was healthy but where it met the frostbitten area, it was pink as a baby's cheek. The rotting flesh had shrunk to about half the width of the healthy part of his fingers, as if a noose had been slipped over them and choked them off. The remnant of each frostbitten finger was shriveled in spikes the color of eggplant. On the index finger of Sutton's left hand, the rotted flesh already had sloughed away, leaving the blunt stub behind.

"This is what happens, Will. The dead flesh falls away. The good stays and your blood will keep it healthy. The natural process is almost complete, I'd say a couple more weeks."

"That one's already's done," Sutton said. "You're gonna saw off the rest, ain't you, Doc?"

"I have some tools. I'll need a bench and a clean cloth. We can't use the hut?"

"No. Ain't no place for doctorin'. We going to use the barn bench."

"Get a clean cloth then and put the water on to boil. Can you get your girl to help?"

"No."

Sutton went to the hut and stoked the fire noisily. The poker rattled loudly, and he banged the lifter for good measure. He took the bandana from the shelf. He told Almy to stay by her bed and not come out.

The child said softly, "What you gonna do, Pa?"

"Just a chat with the doctor and he's gonna take care of these fingers."

Sutton went outside and said, "Over this way, Doc."

He motioned him toward the barn. He went to the bench by the open passageway. When the Doc set his bag on the bench, Sutton removed the bandana and lay it on the bench. Bronson looked at it and then at Sutton, whose face was backlighted by the sunlight through the barn opening.

"My question for ya, Doc. It's this: What went on in your office with Almy? I heard her tell me, and we had a nice talk. So right now, you're gonna tell me. What'd ya do to my little girl?"

Bronson snickered at the man before him. He took Sutton's wrists and lifted both hands to his eyes and held them. The light showed the colors of rot and waste. Sutton's hands held steady, and his thick wrists were firm in the doctor's soft fingers. The doctor's hands trembled when he spoke in a mocking tone with sneers drawn on his tight lips and words pushed through his clenched teeth.

"That girl told you? A girl but twelve years old? Knowing nothing about her own little body? She told you, and you think that's right? A girl whose mother is locked up in the insane asylum? The little girl whose Pa is a pathetic sodbuster in no man's land? You sure you got the story straight, Sutton?"

As he spoke the last words and came to Sutton's name, the doctor's voice raised like a fiery preacher scolding his congregation. Sutton's limp hands flopped in the doctor's grip, the black and yellow tips swirling like paint in the light. The doctor suddenly threw the man's hands toward the sod floor of the barn as if they were dirty gloves.

When he turned to step away he felt the blow to his head and slumped to the ground. When he recoiled and tried to push himself to his feet, Sutton loomed above him.

"You bastard," the doctor yelled, and barely got the words out before Sutton fell upon him. His blackened fingers found the doctor's neck and dug quickly beneath his tight collar and lodged deeply in the flesh as he squeezed harder and harder, the tips piercing the fleshy neck. The doctor kicked violently but could not escape the grip and Sutton only drove his fingers deeper into the neck.

When the kicking stopped and the blood stopped and the face turned bluish and the doctor's tongue pushed through his relaxed jaw, Sutton still dug. Blood leaked inchoately from the punctures in the doctor's neck and still Sutton gripped.

Sutton held beyond being sure. Held beyond time.

Almy said softly, "Pa." She repeated louder, "Pa. Pa!"

She sobbed and lay herself across Sutton's back and beat on him. She could feel his tense muscles drawn. He seemed inanimate, like bronze cast in a murderous pose. He did not hear, could not hear.

And then slowly, like a diver coming to the water's surface, he heard and relaxed. He loosened his grip and extracted his fingers. He rose and as he did Almy stepped back. She looked at the doctor's neck and could see the holes there and the thickening blood seeping from them.

Sutton backed away. His senses returned. He collected himself and saw what he had done. The body lay in the open passageway, and the sunlight poured onto the anguished face of the dead doctor, his blue eyes bulging and bloodshot and staring but not seeing the bright sky.

Sutton looked at the hands that had avenged his pain, holding them before him as if they didn't belong to him, as if he held something else. When his eyes came to the tips, he saw small drops of blood easing only slightly from the stubs where the black tips had been and were no more.

A stillness came over the entry, and breezes stalled. Grasses stilled, and birds and waterfowl vanished. Pond water smoothed like glass, and somewhere on the shore in absolute silence a bull snake wound through the reeds, its length bulged with a kangaroo rat.

28

The burial

EVEN BEFORE morning his fingers had begun to heal, as if no more than a hangnail. He woke early and went outside for chips to kindle a fire in the stove. He boiled water, poured some in a tin cup with nettles, and used the rest to boil a potato.

Almy rose at the same moment and worked with her father in silence. There was a peace about the sod home. They opened the door to the hut and let it stand, and the sunlight painted a warm swash across the dirt floor.

The body still lay on the barn door dirt, the feet inside and the torso in the open air. The kangaroo rats had begun to pick at it. The crows saw the activity and joined in, going first for the still blue eyes. When Dimon rode into the yard on Rootes' black mule, the crows rose and cawed above him as if confronting a competitor.

"Hello! Sutton! Heah!"

Sutton and Almy heard the call and went to the door.

"There is news, Sutton. Have you seen the doctor?"

The question snapped him into the moment, and he flashed the previous day's events as if gazing through a stereo viewer.

"He was here."

"Saw him on the road, Sutton. Wondered if he came here."

Sutton held up his hands to show the change and Dimon knew the doctor was involved.

"Has he gone?"

"I need your help, Dimon. Almy and I need your help."

Dimon dismounted and the three of them went to the doorway of the barn.

"Good Jesus!" Dimon said.

"He's no damn good, Dimon."

"Jesus!"

Almy turned away, and Sutton told her to return to the hut. She started then returned, holding her father's sleeve. He pushed her away and ordered her again to the hut, but she stayed.

"They'll be looking for him, Dimon. Will ya help me do something with this?"

Dimon surveyed the body, Sutton's drooped shoulders, and paced the path from barn to hut and back. He started to say something, then left it, walked more.

"I know a pace,"

They would go now, he said. He told Sutton to wrap the body in burlap and then he saw a skid near the barn and said they could use that. He told him to get a shovel, and then he helped Sutton drag the body onto the skid. Almy came from the hut, paused at the activity, then pitched in.

They secured the body to the skid, and Sutton saddled his horse. He fashioned a sling at each edge of the skid, then knotted a lariat to the sling and secured the other end to the saddle horn. He went to the barn, got a shovel, and tied it to the skid. Dimon mounted his mule and lifted Almy behind him. The procession moved down the lane and out to the road then turned south to catch the rutted road to Oshkosh.

The arm sun moved midway in the sky, and the three of them lumbered on. When the skid bumped over a wash, the load loosened and fell to the sand. They halted the horse and mule and dismounted. The three of them pushed and pulled the cargo back onto the skid and re-tied the lashes, extra tight. Then they mounted and moved ahead again and felt warm in the sun.

They came to the rise and Dimon said "Halt!" and the procession stopped.

"It's there, down there. Cain't quite see it, but it's there." He studied the terrain below and then looked to the south.

"The other'n is down yonder, but we want this way," and he pointed west.

Sutton and Almy sat quietly, asking nothing because Dimon seemed sure this was the answer. Then the old man said, There it is, and they nudged the animals down the slope and through the grasses until Dimon thought he saw the faint trail. He turned the procession and went the way of the trail. For a time, and Dimon didn't know how far, they continued.

Sutton said, Where? and Dimon said, Not yet.

They tuned their senses to the sand and the wind, and no one spoke. Gusts pushed from behind. Dimon turned his eyes left and right, even turned on the mule and looked behind, but then moved straight on, Almy clinging to his back. He loosed the reins and let the animal nose through the grass. Then the mule stopped, and the others behind it. Dimon spurred the animal, but it didn't move. He insisted again, but the animal stalled. He dismounted, and the mule's huge ears turned back, toward him. Then the mule pivoted to the north, stopped and stiffened, like a hunting dog.

"It's here somewhere," Dimon said.

He helped Almy down, and Sutton backed his horse to loosen the tow. He dropped the reins and the horse held in ground tie. The three of them walked each their own way around the area, surveying. The wind stopped, dead quiet all around. Dimon said, "It's here."

Sutton and Almy looked and saw nothing.

"It's where they buried 'im. He's here; no damn marker or nuthin'," he said.

Sutton said, "Who?"

"The black settler. They killed 'im. Deast's men. Mercy Man put 'im here. Know he did. No one knows of this spot."

"Rootes is here?"

"Somewhere. Don't know. Mercy Man took care of it. Left me on the hill watchin' the other burial."

"Other burial?"

"Rootes choked 'im. Deserved it, too."

"Who?"

"Don't know. Never saw 'im. Deast put 'em up to it. Wanted me to take 'em to Rootes Jackson. They got 'im all right, and more than they bargained for."

"You said Rootes is dead."

"He's dead and gone and layin' somewhere here in this here draw."

"I don't see anything like a grave around here."

"Me neither, but that black man's here, Sutton. I know it."

Almy stood by the skid. She watched the conversation seesaw and said nothing. She surveyed the valley and wondered why the Mercy Man came here and if there was something special about the place, but it looked like all the other hills and draws around her home. She wondered what had happened out here. Maybe this place Dimon took them was best.

Sutton got the shovel and began to dig. He scooped the hole, orienting it north and south. When he had finished, they tied the lariat around the doctor's boots and dragged the body into the grave and covered it with sand. They stomped the mound down with their feet, all three of them, working until the trace of the grave was smoothed and the body compacted in sand. For good measure, they pulled the skid across it and smoothed it more.

They wound their work down as a clock might slow, finally pausing at once and looking around the place. Almy said, Look, Pa, and she pointed toward the water. They saw a small pond, more of the marsh where the ground water touched the surface. Chokecherries grew beside it, and Sutton said, "My god. Chokecherries."

Dimon said, "Them's chokecherries all right, but they ain't set yet. Just blooms."

Sutton said, "It's where the Cheyenne stayed the rough winter, years ago, maybe in the seventies. I heard Coulson tell of it."

They remounted and left the spot quietly, as if family leaving a church service. When they had regained the top of the hill and turned north on the rutted road, Sutton said, "Good god, you helped me, Dimon."

"It's good," the old man said. "It's good."

29

Agents close in

"HE MIGHT be dead."

Elias Hunter was not pleased when he heard it.

"When?"

Ruhoff hesitated. He had answers, much information. But not everything was clear. He needed convincing evidence, no room to wiggle. He knew the sentiment locally was with the cattle interests; they had the most money, the most power, the most influence. There was no room for ambivalence. His case must be conclusive, airtight.

"I don't know. The settler Dimon said Rootes Jackson was killed by some of Deast's men. But the old man's a little crazy. I don't know if he's right about this or not."

"Well, we need to figure that out. What can we do?"

"Dimon says he was taken captive and ordered to lead Deast's men to Jackson's settlement south, toward Oshkosh. He says they happened upon Jackson along the road and when Jackson resisted, they shot him."

"Is there a body?"

"None that I can locate."

"Dimon doesn't know where?"

"He says he can't recall, but I think he's hiding something."

"What?"

"I don't know. Nothing he'd like better than to put Deast away for fencing and threatening him. But I think he knows something else he's not telling."

"You know this."

"No, I think it. I'll keep on him."

"Mr. Ruhoff, do you have enough for a case before Judge Munger?"

"We have the testimony of Dimon on threats, and now he's adding a murder. He says he saw them shoot Jackson. He says it's Deast's men, not Deast. We don't have any tie to Deast concerning the murder, if there was one. There's no body."

"And the fencing?"

"We have plenty on that. I've been out there with the claim locator, Coulson. There are plenty of illegal fences, and no sign of removing any of them. I can testify to that, and Coulson is a fine witness. We can bring a civil case. Whether the judge does anything about it is another matter. But I have substantiated that the fences are illegally on homesteader claims."

Very many of them?"

"Lord, yes. Very many of them. Mr. Hunter, sir, many details are left to be discovered, but I would not be surprised if there is a hundred thousand, maybe two hundred thousand acres that are illegally fenced."

"Hundreds of thousands?"

"Yes, sir."

"Same operators?"

"There are some big ones; there are some smaller ones. Deast Land and Cattle is the biggest around here. But he isn't operating alone."

"Who else then -- fencing, I mean?"

"Some smaller cattle companies. Deast is the biggest."

"And who is helping Deast?"

"Deast and his hired hands seem to handle the illegal fencing on their own. The intimidation -- that's another matter. I need more information, but one person seems clearly involved."

"Yes...?"

"The local doctor. His name is Bronson. I have no doubt he is involved."

"Anyone else?"

"The county attorney, and possibly the sheriff. Sheriff Brier."

"Fencing?"

"No; Deast has his men to do that. I mean intimidation. I've heard that the Board of Insanity may have been used and Bronson and some of the other cattlemen are in on that."

"How?"

"If threats and intimidation don't work, they will haul in a settler and determine he's insane. Ship him off to the asylum in Hastings or Omaha. Sometimes they work on the spouse or a child -- they use any way of scaring the entrymen away."

Hunter placed the tips of his fingers lightly together and sat thinking. The lobby of the Rackett Hotel was quiet, and the bellman stood attentively and silent. The desk clerk busied himself with papers and room keys. Hunter leaned forward slowly and engaged Ruhoff's eyes.

"You have evidence of misuse of the Insanity Board?"

"Nothing provable. Insanity is subjective. There was a man in Garden County sent away by the board and then released by the asylum. They didn't see any insanity. It may have been malicious, maybe not."

Hunter seemed perplexed and uneasy.

"We will proceed with the fencing charges. We'll file in district court and hope for the best with Judge Munger. We'll make sure the newspapers have it, and folks can know we mean business out here."

Hunter seemed satisfied with his decision. Smug. Then he said, "We need to make an example of Deast. The illegal fencing won't stop out here until people come to understand they can't just take government land and put it to their own uses. Roosevelt is disappointed; he thinks more should be done about wrongful enclosures. We'll put this issue in Munger's lap and push him to respond appropriately. The criminal matters can't be successfully prosecuted, if you're correct that evidence is insufficient."

Then he added, "Anything else I should know?"

"Well, sir, there are several entries that appear to be held by soldiers or their widows who live in homes in Omaha or Grand Island."

"The soldiers' credit?"

"They get credit for time served in the military, and for some it means the prove-up is nearly done before entry begins."

"Fraudulent entries?"

"It appears so, sir. Why else would a widow in Omaha or an old soldier in Grand Island file on a Kincaid?"

30

Where's Doc Bronson?

HIS OFFICE was locked tight, and folks in Rackett were beginning to wonder if Doc Bronson had left in the middle of the night. It wasn't like him, they said, but other folks had surely tired of the hard life in a small town in the Nebraska Sand Hills. Maybe he just pulled up and went back East.

Jonas Buck got word of it and went by to look for himself. Then he went for Brier and the two of them took stock of the situation and decided to enter by force. The sheriff used his bar to pry the door open, and when they looked around, the office looked normal, no sign of a struggle. Folks began to gather on the boardwalk, and peer in the windows.

"What's happened to Doc?" said Ruthie Kremlacek. For the town gossip, this was big news, and she hoped to get in on the details and then head to the market, as she did every day. Others with her said it was nothing; Doc just wasn't at the office this morning, wasn't seen around town yesterday either, and the day before that. Maybe it had been a week since anybody saw him. Some patients were upset, needed a doctor, impatient.

"Why don't they just check his house," Ruthie asked, and someone said, well, they've surely already done that. And the saloon, too, just in case. Nothing over there either. Maybe he rode out for a house call.

Inside Buck and Sheriff Brier sorted through the Doc's desk and found his appointment book. The last entry said, "Sutton."

"Good God," Buck said. "I hope he didn't ride out there." They reasoned that Widlund may know something about it, and when they stepped out of the doctor's office to go next door, the editor was on the boardwalk with the others.

"What's all the commotion, Jonas?"

"Well, no one's seen Doc in a couple of days," Buck said. "His last appointment says he went out to see your brother-in-law. You've heard something?"

Ruthie spoke up, "They say Will Sutton was here in the doctor's office a few days ago. Let's see, now, that was last Tuesday. Or was it Wednesday? What did I tell you, Agnes?" and she turned to the lady next to her. Millie Foster said You said it was last week, Ruthie. And Agnes said that was right, she remembered Ruthie saying so.

Widlund sidestepped the gossiping women and spoke directly to Buck.

"How long has he gone missing?"

"Maybe a week. Not sure. I figur he was away to Hastings or something. He takes off occasionally, so maybe he'll show."

With the chatter buzzing around him, Widlund stood quietly. In his head, he reviewed Sutton's stay at his home. He thought about the handkerchief. He worried Sutton was upset by it. Sutton left abruptly the next morning and he had not heard from him since. When they heard nothing, they assumed he'd had the amputation done and gone back to Almy. Now, with the Doc gone missing, Widlund could not help but wonder if Sutton was somehow involved.

"You say his appointment book showed a visit to Sutton's place?"

"Just said 'Sutton.' If he hasn't returned by morning, Sheriff and I will go out and talk to him. Maybe Sutton or somebody else saw him."

Widlund said he'd go with them, but Buck said he'd be with the sheriff, and they'd take a deputy, too. Widlund nodded his agreement and asked the sheriff to keep him posted on the developments. He pushed through the small crowd and headed back to his office.

Elias Hunter was waiting, indifferent to the commotion outside.

"Is something wrong," Elias Hunter asked.

"Good morning, sir. The doctor hasn't been around for a few days, so folks have begun to worry. Probably he'll turn up. It's just that at the moment, no one knows where he is."

"Well, I hope he's all right. Excuse me, Mr. Widlund, but I wonder if I might have a word with you."

Widlund offered him a chair. His mind was on Sutton and the mountain of work ahead of him, but he gathered himself and asked Hunter what was on his mind. When Hunter told him that charges had been filed in U.S. District Court alleging thirty-seven counts of illegal fencing against Deast Land and Cattle Co. of Rackett, Nebraska, he reached for his notebook.

"And I wonder if you've any information to offer to me."

Widlund looked up from his notes.

"I don't know what you mean, sir."

"I have reliable information that there are other activities in this country that are beyond civil matters. I have reason to believe there may be criminal activity as well, including threats and intimidation. Maybe even a shooting. Have you heard of any of this?"

Widlund paused long. He fidgeted in his chair as his eyes darted from his notes to Hunter's face, to the window and back to Hunter's face. He was careful with his response.

"I believe my sister-in-law was quickly sent away to an insane asylum in Hastings. I think the motive was to pressure my brother-in-law to abandon his homestead. I believe they want his homestead because it fits into their plans for their cattle ranch. I'm sorry, sir, but that is what I suspect."

Hunter wore a satisfied smile. He was on the brink of a professional breakthrough. His career could be advanced in Washington if he could return with verdicts against the men who defrauded the government. The president himself wanted the homestead provisions enforced. Hunter hoped for reward, possibly a promotion or a political career of his own.

"Who is your sister-in-law?"

Widlund hesitated. He had the interests of his family, and the interests of his business to consider. The cattlemen not only controlled the wealth on the prairie, but they were widely respected. Homesteaders had nothing and could wield little influence. If the federal government was interested in helping them, then the cattlemen were the opponent. Especially for a newspaperman, it could be delicate to be forced to align with one interest or the other.

Still, it was family. He couldn't cross Mildred. She would want the best for Maddie, but she would want the newspaper to do well, too. What if he were a witness in a federal case against Deast Land and Cattle? His preference was to remain on the outside, a reporter and editor and businessman, not a witness.

"She is Maddie Sutton. She and her husband have filed for entry on a Kincaid south of here," he said.

"And she has been committed you say?"

"She has, to Hastings. But she is not insane. She suffered a very traumatic personal loss, and it affected her judgment noticeably. She lived with us for a time and was improving. I am convinced that her erratic behavior was only temporary and would get better with the support of family. But they came to our door and demanded that she report for an inquiry."

Hunter wondered how it could be proved that she was wrongly committed. Insanity is subjective; there can only be the judgment of someone else.

"Has anything been done in her behalf at the asylum?"

"We have done nothing yet. I am in the process of writing to the administrator and asking him to review Maddie's case. I am not optimistic. I'm sure they get many appeals; many families want their relative released. But we have decided as a family to make a request."

Hunter agreed by nodding slightly and pursing his lips, as if he had a plan.

"Was her behavior unusual?"

"She lost a daughter to the blizzard. She was devastated by it. She found the little girl frozen to death. People saw her change and wondered if something was wrong."

"In that case, sir, the Insanity Board may have done the right thing."

"They will argue that, of course. But we were seeing improvement. Sometimes people are just badly shocked, but they adjust and return to normal."

"Who is on the Insanity Board?"

"The ones I fear are Doc Bronson and the county attorney Buck, Jonas Buck."

"No cattlemen?"

"Two, sir. Yi Yi Jorgensen and Deast."

Hunter now smiled openly. If there were others committed to the asylum with less evidence of insanity, perhaps a case could be made. Maddie Sutton may not represent the clearest case, but it was a good case to know about. He thanked Widlund for his bravery to disclose a delicate family matter then rose to go.

"There is something else, Mr. Hunter. Two things, actually."

"Tell me."

"First, I intend to report your activities here in my newspaper. People need to know. I thank you for the interview and will proceed with a story for the next issue. If there is anything else that you care to add, I urge you to talk to me very soon."

Hunter said, "And the second?"

"You will want to check into several Kincaid filings in this area that may be in the names of old soldiers or widows of old soldiers. I can recommend one filing that has me suspicious. The name is Tomppert."

Hunter put on his hat and extended his hand for a parting shake.

"We are aware of that one, sir, and I think you will want to report about it when the time comes."

31

Widlund seeks counsel

WIDLUND MADE made it to the porch but didn't go inside. He put his case by the side table and fell into the wicker rocker. As the sun dipped yellow, the neighbors' homes, most of them painted white, turned the color of old newsprint. He admired the sharp contrast of the shadows. He thought to try painting them some day. Light, when it comes from the side as it does on clear evenings, has more character than mid-day light, he thought, more suitable to the artist. For contrast, he pictured the summer sun at noon, shining straight down, and he decided the harsh, direct light can be oppressive. Odd, he thought; sometimes the best light isn't the brightest.

Mildred appeared at the door with a drink. He took a tiny amount on his lips and tongue.

"Whiskey and the tart minerals of Nebraska groundwater," he said. "Thank you."

She kissed him on his forehead then moved gracefully behind him to rub his neck. He let his head fall and wondered if he could just pour out his brain and let its ideas rest in her loving hands. She felt his response and let her hands stop. She remained still for the moment, and Widlund sighed deeply. She kissed him again, on top of his head this time, then released and sat in the other rocker.

"The doctor is gone. No one knows where."

"Ruthie came by," she said.

Widlund laughed deliberately.

"My main competitor," he said.

"There's that. And the federal government stopped by again."

His brown hair, ruffled from her caresses, added to his deflated look. She reached across and smoothed it with her fingers, renewing the part and pushing the hair away from his eyes. He turned like a child and let her fret over him. His mustache had grown bushy in recent days, lacking attention. The whiskers fell from his nostrils, covered his top lip, and hid his mouth. His angular nose separated his usually intense eyes, which softened as the evening arrived. His bow tie was loosened and his collar open.

"Ruthie said people are worried about Doc," she said. "I'm worried about Will. He left here abruptly."

She thought about the possibilities. If something had happened in the doctor's office, the evidence would be clear.

"Did anyone go inside?"

"Doc's office? Sure. Sheriff and his sidekick, Buck."

"What turned up?"

"It looked in order. They found his appointment book. He wrote in it that he would go to Will's."

"He said he'd have the Doc take off his fingers," Mildred said."

"Maybe something happened on the way."

Mildred rose and went inside. Widlund sipped the drink and thought about the story he would write about the interview with Hunter. He already had decided to put the story out front. He'd mostly use the quotes he scribbled down. He would follow up with an editorial, maybe the following edition. His headline would be straightforward, "Agents to

Enforce Fencing Rules." A subhead could explain that the story was based on an interview with a U.S. Attorney.

Then he wondered what would turn up with the doctor. It probably would blow over; Doc probably just went off for an adventure, maybe into the Dakotas or Wyoming.

What was Will thinking? Maybe he should not have told him about Viola's bandana. Maybe he should have kept quiet. Regardless, Widlund was beginning to fear he bore responsibility.

Mildred returned with her tatting. She spread the work on her lap, smoothing the knotted fabric with her hands. Widlund watched; he admired her various skills. She was capable of many things completely foreign to him. He wasn't putting it to words, but the thought crossed his mind again that he felt very fortunate to have both a wife and a talented, smart friend.

"OK; I have a question for you," he said. She looked up from her work and smiled.

"What if Will did something? He's got a heap of trouble already. Would you think I should have kept quiet about the bandana? I wonder if I should have shut up."

"You did what you thought was best. That's enough – for me.

"Darn!" she said suddenly.

He looked up at the exclamation. She held up the tatting to examine the small mistake. As she did, he noticed her slender fingers, long and thin. Her nails were trimmed and the cuticles pushed back and healthy. He thought her hands could not have been prettier if they had been sculpted.

"It must be the light. I can't see what I'm doing," she said.

She gathered her project and rose to go inside.

"You going to stay here for a while?"

"No; I'll be along," he said.

The door banged shut, pulled by the long black spring attaching it to the door frame. The light was almost gone, and he felt he should go in, too. But he sat in thought: Viola, Maddie, Hunter, Doc, the newspaper stories he must write, the ads he must sell.

He sipped the final drops of his drink then rose. As he pulled the door open, he looked back at the shadowy homes and faint businesses. The sun was down, and the dim grey itself was fading.

32

Sutton has visitors

JONAS BUCK looked down at the trampled sand in front of Sutton's hut. His mare stood calmly as Sheriff Brier reined his animal alongside. The two wore town clothes – felt hats, neckties, wool coats - as if headed for court. Brier's badge bulged from his vest, and his holstered Colt 45 was held in place by a leather strap snapped tightly behind the hammer. Both carried rifles in leather scabbards, Brier's plain as a fencepost and Buck's carved with floral patterns.

Sutton stood in the doorway. The creases in his leathery cheeks were rigid as stone. His head was bare, and his brown hair fell in greasy waves, except for a jagged cowlick that waved from the back of his head. His bare feet jutted like weathered floorboards from his frayed pants. His eyes were dark in the doorway shadow. The morning summer sun bathed the hills in golden warmth. A breeze whipped the grasses in the distance, and a meadowlark sang from the top of the barn.

"How are your fingers?"

Buck probed cautiously. He looked more at Brier than at Sutton when he spoke. The sheriff quickly echoed.

"Yeah, Sutton, how're them fingers?"

He stood still, no change in expression, no change in his stance. He lifted both hands, palms in, and Buck and Brier could see the pink flesh. Remaining bits of pale yellow rot spotted the tips. All the black was gone.

"I guess Doc musta helped clean 'em up," Brier said. "Doc out here to help?"

"I haven't seen the Doc 'cept when I was in town days ago. These here fingers fell off by themselves."

"That's funny, Sutton. We thought Doc came out here. We saw in his book that he had an appointment with you. We figured that was out here. He's been missing quite a few days now."

"Ain't seen 'im," Sutton said.

Almy came to the door and stood by her Pa. She wore dirty coveralls, her hair knotted. Splotches of grime contrasted with her fair skin. She, too, wore no shoes. She looked at the two men on the horses towering above her. Jonas Buck tipped his hat, but she said nothing. She moved behind her Pa and peered from behind his chest.

The sheriff dismounted and ground-tied his horse. He came close to Sutton and the girl and made an unconvincing tip of his hat. Sutton inched back defensively, into the doorway, and Almy moved with him.

"Not sure what yer business is here," Sutton said. "If you need some water, you help yourself to that there in the cistern. I got work to do, so I'd be agreeable if you'd move on."

"We have a few questions, for you, Mr. Sutton."

"You're already askin' plenty of questions, Mr. Buck. Maybe you can come to your point."

The sheriff moved in closer, and Sutton didn't move. He slowly raised his arm palm out and put his hand to the sheriff's chest and the stubs covered the badge. The sheriff halted and didn't resist. Buck watched from his horse.

"You just stay where you are, Sheriff. You're puttin' a scare into my Almy here. There's no need."

"We're going to take you to town, Sutton," Buck said. "Sheriff here needs you to come along. We need some answers about Doc."

"Told ya, I haven't seen 'im."

"Is that right, miss? You and your Pa haven't seen Doc Bronson? Your Pa's fingers fell off without the Doc's help? You say that's right, miss?"

"Listen, Buck. You leave the girl alone."

Almy moved forward, aside her Pa. She started quietly, "Pa's right ..."

Sutton put his hand on her shoulder and drew her in.

"S'all right, Almy. No need."

Buck said, "You put your shoes on, both of you. Mr. Sutton, Sheriff Brier is going to put some binders on you, and we're taking you to Rackett. You are under arrest for the disappearance of Doc Bronson. We'll keep you until you tell us what you know about where Doc is."

Sutton went in quietly and Almy stood at the door. Brier stepped back, waiting. Buck sat his horse. They could hear Sutton gathering some things inside and waited. He came to the door, knelt and put on his shoes, tying the frayed laces, too short to catch all the eyelets. He told Almy to go put on her shoes, and she went inside. She did the same, then stood and looked to Sutton. He said he'd get one more thing and went back inside. When he returned to the door, he was carrying his rifle, and he pushed down and then up on the lever and the cartridge clicked into place. He leveled the rifle slowly at Buck, and when the sheriff stepped toward him, he turned quickly, and the barrel pointed directly at the sheriff's badge.

"You all best get off my property," Sutton said.

The sheriff froze, and Buck's horse fidgeted. Almy's eyes darted from sheriff to Buck. She did not look at her father.

"Now, Sutton," Buck said. "Let's be reasonable. We can talk ..."

"You took my Ma!" Almy screamed.

The lark startled and flew. Buck's horse lurched back.

"She's not crazy! You and Doc Bronson took her! You get her back!"

She rushed to Brier and pounded her fists on his chest. He kept his arms at his side and didn't resist. She continued to beat him, flailing her arms, and yelling. Soon, she cried and stopped the beating, fell to her knees and wept. Sutton moved behind her and with the rifle still pointed at the sheriff and his stubby index finger alongside the trigger, put his left hand under her shoulder and lifted her abruptly. When he did, the sheriff moved quickly and flicked away the rifle with his left hand as his right fist caught Sutton in the neck. The rifle fell and discharged but the load hit no one.

Buck bolted from his horse and held Sutton from behind. Sutton struggled and freed himself, but the sheriff drew his sidearm and fired a shot into the air. Then he put the gun to Sutton's neck and ordered him to lie down in the dirt, and he did. On her knees, Almy backed into the doorway.

Buck drew his sidearm and held it to Sutton's head. Brier pulled Sutton's arms behind him and put on the cuffs. Brier looped a rope over Sutton's head and around his chest. Then he mounted his horse and wrapped the rope twice around the horn. Buck took the girl and lashed her likewise to his saddle.

Screaming, Almy said, "That Doctor deserved to die!"

Buck halted his horse and dismounted. He walked to the girl and stooped his head to her level. He said quietly, "Doc deserved to die, didn't he?" and Almy sobbed and shook her head up and down in agreement.

Sutton said quietly, "That's enough now, Almy."

Buck said, "And your daddy killed him, didn't he?" and he rose quickly as he said it loudly. "He killed 'im, didn't he?"

Almy looked at the ground and said nothing more. Buck demanded loudly, "Your daddy killed the Doc, didn't he!"

Almy looked up to her Pa and then into the narrowed eyes of the county attorney. She said in a murmur, "He was mean," and she began to weep again.

33

U.S. indicts Deast Land and Cattle

ELIAS HUNTER and Rodney Ruhoff sat in stiff chairs in the staid office of District Judge W. H. Munger in Omaha. With them was U. S. Attorney Irving W. Baxter, a thin man with wire glasses and slick hair. He was eager to come to the point; he had a speech to make at noon before the Nebraska Bar Association.

Baxter said the indictments were in order. The judge reviewed the docket with his clerk and trial date was set for mid-July.

"The government alleges, sir, that the Deast interests have illegally fenced 4,500 acres. We will argue for full prosecution of these enclosures, sir," Baxter said.

"I'm sure you will, Mr. Baxter, and the court welcomes the hearing."

"We do not believe that the practice of illegal fencing is limited to the relatively small number of acres with which the indictments concern themselves. We believe there are far more acres the cattle interests have fenced."

Judge Munger peered over the reading lenses perched at the tip of his nose and sniffed at Baxter as if the remark were inappropriate. He rifled through the papers before him, then leaned back in his chair.

"Mr. Baxter, how is the settlement going out there? It has been my impression that the homesteaders are having a deuce of a time of it. What is your understanding?"

"I am not the best to say, your honor. Mr. Hunter and Mr. Ruhoff knows better than I."

"Well, gentlemen? What do you say?"

Hunter nodded to Ruhoff. He said, "I believe you've spent more time there than I have, Mr. Ruhoff."

"It is not easy for them, your honor. The elements are difficult, and the land doesn't take the plow very well."

"The Indians have a saying," the Judge said. "Grass no good upside down."

"The Indians have a point your honor," Ruhoff said.

Ruhoff's surveys of the land, his contact with the locater, Coulson, and the conditions at homesteads he saw supported his doubt that farmers ever would make it. But it wasn't up to him; the law gave the homesteaders entry rights, and most were willing to see through the hardships before them.

"The Kincaids will make a difference, sir. The chances are better with a section. Cattle can be run, and hay can be grown in some of the bottoms."

"Kincaid pushed hard for the change, and the Republicans came around. A section is a lot of land to come by ... as a gift," the judge said.

"Meaning no disrespect, sir," Ruhoff said, "but the land is not a gift. Five years of residence plus improvements is a heavy price for some of the 'steaders."

"Well, thank you for your perspective, Mr. Ruhoff."

"There's another factor," Ruhoff said, eyeing Baxter and Hunter. "These indictments tell of harassment, intimidation. As they show, we are prepared to prosecute the intimidation, sir. Regardless of the outcome of the Kincaiders, it is hard enough for them without threats by cattle interests, in my opinion."

"Certainly, my boy. And the courtroom is the place to settle these matters, isn't it?"

None of them responded. They thanked the judge and said their goodbyes. In the hallway, Baxter excused himself and hurried off for his luncheon engagement.

Hunter said, "Our prospects look dim, Rodney."

"I'm afraid so, sir. The judge doesn't seem eager to make an example of the cattlemen if they're going to win out anyway."

"I agree. The president will not be pleased. Interior Secretary Hitchcock is under a great deal of pressure from him. Heads will roll if this case isn't prosecuted fully, I'm afraid."

"Yes sir," Ruhoff said. "Heads will roll."

34

The news hits the Omaha paper

FROSTY NEWTON was in the holding area of the Omaha jail on suspicion of chicken theft when he picked up a frayed copy of the Bee that someone had thrown to the detainees with vague hopes of keeping them quiet.

He saw the headline. The din around him made it hard to concentrate. One old boy, in for public drunkenness, loudly yelled that "them sonnabitches can flame in hell" so Newton moved as far as he could and turned his shoulder into the corner of the cell while he read.

Cattlemen fined, sentenced to 'jail' for illegal fences

He glanced quickly through the text and saw the name of his former employer, so he returned to the top and read on with interest. It was the subhead he saw next:

$200 fine paid, then it's 'time' at Omaha bar

"Good god," Newton said out loud. "A bar?"

The story said his former boss, Rutherford G. Deast, and two of his business partners at Deast Land and Cattle were sentenced in U.S. District Court for illegally fencing thousands of acres near Rackett. The first paragraph read:

U.S. District Judge W. H. Munger yesterday fined three western Nebraska cattlemen $200 and sentenced them to six hours in custody for illegally fencing more than 200,000 acres of western Nebraska land belonging to the federal government.

"Son of a bitch!" Newton said out loud when he read that Judge Munger's idea of punishment, besides the fine, was six hours in custody of a U.S. Marshal who watched over Deast and his partners while they sipped drinks at the Riverview Lounge at the Omaha Grand Hotel. The gentlemen were seen serving their 'terms' seated in the leather wingback chairs at the poshest bar in Omaha.

When he finally had his own day in court, Newton decided to speak out when he had the chance. He said he knew things about these cattlemen that somebody ought to know, and that his small crime was nothing compared to what these men were doing out in the Sand Hills.

The judge was no stranger to stories told by the desperate men and women who came before him for sentencing, and when Newton was finally done with his speech, the judge fined him two dollars and sentenced him to eighteen nights in the Omaha jail, with credit for time served.

If Newton had two dollars, he would have bought chicken for dinner in the first place, rather than try to steal it. He made that case to the judge as well, and this time the judge, probably weary from a long day of listening to desperate no-counts, waived the fine and ordered him to hard labor for five more days.

At least the county fed and sheltered him, but those five days etched in Newton's head like text on a headstone. There was no justice in it that he could see. What was at work as far as he could understand it was a rich man getting off easy while a poor bastard such as he had one thing after another flung at him.

What's more, in his own mind he wasn't a bad man, just down on his luck. When he thought back on it, Deast had sent him to find and kill a man, a black man by the way, because he had the nerve to stand up to Deast's bullying. Deast would stop at nothing to get what he wanted.

As Newton saw it, his own error was owing to his empty stomach. No one was hurt, unless you counted the loss of chickens, but a man's got to eat, and a settin' hen and a healthy rooster can make more chickens.

As he pounded away at the rocks the guards set before him, the lesson in this sort of justice bore deeper and deeper. When he was finally released, he worked a few odd jobs around Omaha, fed and sheltered himself legally, and even saved a few dollars. He was well short of enough for passenger fare, but he knew how to hop a freight, and the few nickels he had saved would help keep him out of trouble.

His idea was to go to Rackett and tell somebody about what really happened out there, and why that damned Deast was no good. He didn't seem to care, or it didn't occur to him, that taking on Deast in his own territory might be dangerous. He just knew that something ought to be done.

The warm summer nights made his seat in a boxcar almost cozy. When the freight slowed about a mile east of what he figured must be Rackett, he hopped off and walked the rest of the way into town, making sure he avoided the rail police.

A breeze lazed across the hills, and a huge summer moon rose in the east. He had no hurry and no worry either, so he paused a moment to watch. It was amazing, the size of that yellow moon, and he wondered how the moon could be that huge and that yellow when it first rises and then get so small and white when it was high in the sky. It made him think for a second that some things in life are about the same, big and bright as hell at first, but with a little time they get small and become just something else to reckon with.

As he moved along in the moonlight, his own shadow danced ahead of him, and he noticed how thin he looked, and from then on all he could think about was how hungry and thirsty he was. He eventually made it to the edge of town and poked his way around until he found the saloon and went inside. With fifty cents he still had on him, he paid for a plate of potatoes and a slice of bacon to go with three eggs, and topped it all off with a pint of beer.

It was then that Lucy joined him.

"Hey, big fella, know where a girl can get a drink?"

Newton's hand moved to his pocket where his only dollar remained. Broke but hopeful, he talked long enough with Lucy for them both to wonder how far his resources could take him.

"I might find something here for a drink. What's yer name, honey?"

Lucy seized the opening and sat. When her beer came, she slurped it noisily.

"What brings you to Rackett, stranger?"

"Here on business," he said. "I'm here in the name of truth and justice."

As Newton talked, she kept an eye on the door for other prospects.

"I'm all ears, Big Boy. Tell Momma Lucy all your troubles."

"Well, I was working around these parts some time back, and then I left. Wound up in the hoosegow in Omaha, and I didn't like much of what I saw. So now I'm out here to see if I can set a few things straight."

She leaned toward him, and as she expected, his eyes fell. She cocked her head to the left then rocked just a little, and Newton followed the motion with brows raised and his jaw lax.

"Know a man out here who'll damn near do anything to get what he wants," he said.

"Lots of men out here do that," she said with a smile that parted her painted lips and exposed her yellow teeth.

"I ran his cattle and pulled his calves -- fine. Honest work. But the crooked sonofabitch sent me on a dirty errand. Enough, by gawd. I quit him and went to town."

Lucy adjusted her red and black dress and Newton watched, as she knew he would. She put the painted nail of her right index finger under his chin and lifted in gently until his eyes came up, and then she puckered her lips and made a mock kiss.

"Let's have another beer, honey," she said.

The drinks arrived, and the bartender demanded payment. Newton pulled out the last dollar and the bartender disappeared with it. He returned shortly, tossed a quarter on the table, and Lucy wondered how much more was in Newton's pocket.

"A man's got to eat, don't he?" he said.

"Eatin's part of it," she said.

"Yeah. I stole some goddam chickens for dinner, but some kids saw me and told their dad. He came out with a 12-gauge. Jesus!"

Newton slurped his beer and wiped the foam away on his dirty sleeve.

"Ended up in goddam jail," he said.

"Well, you're a free man now, aren't you, honey," she said. "Free to do anything your li'l heart desires ..."

She bent in again. His arm was on the table, and she leaned forward until she rested on it, then wiggled again. She put her hand on his knee.

"Jesus," Newton said.

The bartender arrived again and said to Lucy, "You keeping busy, hon?" She smiled, and he left.

"Saw a man killed out there. Two of 'em. None it for any damn good, either. Just a rich man wantin' his way and no goddam law to keep 'im from it."

Lucy rubbed his knee.

"That's right, honey. You just tell Momma Lucy all about it."

"Hot-headed Irishman with me," he said. "Jesus! And a sawed-off runt who never should left his sow of a mother."

He called the bartender over and ordered a shot of whiskey.

"One shot or two?" the bartender asked.

"Well, two, goddam it. For Chrissake!"

"Say, fella. You got the money to pay, don't you?"

"I got this here quarter. Bring what it'll buy."

"It'll buy a beer and a shot."

"Well, Jesus!" Newton said.

Lucy pulled her hand back from Newton's knee and sat up straight. She looked hard at him and rose to go.

"Naw, don't go, Just sit here a little longer," he said. And she did.

"Got some more to tell Momma Lucy, farm boy?"

"You have the shot, honey. You bein' good to me."

The drinks arrived and Lucy swigged the whiskey.

"Hot-headed Irishman and a sawed-off coward, that's what I was workin' with on this goddam cattlemen's dirty business. Find the black man, he says. We find some goddam homesteader who's supposed to lead us to the black man, and, hell, he's just as innocent as a goddam baby. I let 'im go. Buried the black man and let the old 'steader go."

"It's a good story, cowboy," Lucy said.

"Ain't right. I go to jail for a couple of chickens to fill my belly, and the rich man steals and threatens and pushes everybody around. His pal the judge sends him over to a bar for punishment. Goddam poor idea of law, if you ask me."

"You got any more money, honey?" Lucy said.

"I'm done in," Newton said.

"You been nice knowin'. You keep yourself safe, now." She rose again.

"Hey, can you help me find a place? I need a good sleep."

"I can show you a place you can afford," Lucy said. She led him outside and down the street, then pointed to a barn.

"There's hay in there," she said. "Sleep tight, farm boy."

35

Frosty's tale

NEWTON FOUND the newspaper office the next morning. Pete was at the Linotype.

"Help ya?"

"Yessir. I'd like to see the editor. I have some things to tell 'im."

"He's not here."

"When will he be back?"

"Only the gods know. Why?"

"Said before, got some things to tell 'im."

"You'll have to come back. Maybe two or three. He's plenty busy."

Newton said, "Came all the way from Omaha to see 'im. Reckon I'll just wait."

"You can do that outside, mister."

"You're a friendly one, ain't ya? I'll wait right here in this chair."

"Have it your way but keep quiet. I've got work to do."

Newton seated himself and wondered what sort of operation this newspaper business is. He looked at the mess on Widlund's desk and figured nobody could know what was there. Miracle they ever got anything in print, he thought. He helped himself to a copy of the paper on Widlund's desk, but it was an old edition, from May.

He read it anyway, looking with interest at the ads. He shuffled through the inside pages, poking at the headlines, reading the one-sentence fillers at the bottom of the page, and thinking how hopelessly removed any of it was from a hungry belly that real men tended to.

Back on the first page, though, he read about a homesteader named Sutton who was being held in a murder investigation. He'd heard that name before, and when he read a little further and came across another name he remembered; Dimon.

Both of those were sections Deast wanted. The dead man, so the story said, was a doctor, name of Bronson, and Newton sat straight up in his chair when he read that because Doc had an interest in the Deast operation and was one of the men who told him and Moloney to get the Negro. Doc dead and some 'steader held for it?

An hour passed, and when he was just about to give it up, in walked Widlund. He stood and introduced himself, and the newspaperman looked completely disinterested in a ragged bum of a man who looked to have just crawled out of a hay loft, which was true.

"I'm here to tell you about a man named Deast," Newton said.

"Deast, now. Well, you sit there, and you can tell me all you want," Widlund said.

Newton reviewed his history in the Sand Hills, including the day when the black man was murdered and who done it and why.

"And you saw all of this?"

"I tell you only what I know, no more, sir."

"And what makes you come forward now with all of this?"

"It's not right what I hear is going on. Deast is a crook, might say even evil. He don't mind putting out of his way anyone who gets in it. I told you; he sent me and a couple of his men to round up a 'steader he wanted out of the way, and he had a grudge to settle with a black man. Our orders was to take care of both."

"You realize, certainly you do, that you're implicating yourself here, Mr. Newton?"

"I didn't kill no one," he said.

"But you were the hired gun . . ."

"I was but I guess I'll throw myself on the mercy of the court, 'cause I ain't hurt nobody."

"Except for a kidnapping. That's not working in your favor."

"Guess not, but I spent time in the hoosegow and breaking enough rocks to make me think something's wrong when a man does bad things, pays a token fine and spends his jail time in a bar, per the judge's orders."

To Widlund, the man's story seemed too high-minded for the type of man he was. But he listened, because he concurred about Deast and Doc, and he knew of the light sentence the men had paid for a conviction of fraud on the United States government.

"You know this man Sutton?"

"No more'n what I read in your paper. But I do know that Deast wanted his claim."

"How do you know that?"

"Heard 'im talk about it with the dead man and that attorney, Buck."

"Dead man?"

"The Doc. Bronson."

"I see. How do you know about Doc Bronson?

"Read it in your newspaper."

"The man you kidnapped ... you know him?"

"Just his name. Dimon. I let 'im go."

"Why?"

"I'd had enough. Jesus!"

"Where are the dead men buried?"

"I saw the black man come out of a sandhill valley and when I had his body on my hands, I figured to put him back in there. Nobody like to find it, off'n the road and tucked in the hills, a grove of chokecherries hidin' it."

"And you know where he's buried? You could find that again?"

"Believe I could, yes."

"Where's the other dead man?"

"Not sure. "Didn't do the buryin'. Lonnie did that part."

"Lonnie?"

"Lonie Moloney, Deast's other hired gun. He was with me that day, like I told ya."

Widlund rose from his chair and paced. He stood over Newton and looked at him carefully. The man was rough, but he didn't look to be a liar.

"You know the man held for murdering Doc Bronson is my brother-in-law?"

Newton ran his fingers through his long white hair shaking his head negative.

"He done it? He kilt the Doc?"

"He hasn't been tried. I don't know. There's no body. No one knows where Doc is, or whether he's dead or alive. He's no doubt missing, though."

"What'd Doc do to him?"

"Nothing to do with his homestead, Mr. Newton. Nothing to do with that business."

"Well, what then? What you think?"

"I think Bronson was an evil man, and if he's dead, he deserved to die. Don't know that Will Sutton has it in him to do that. He's a hard-working man. Honest and good to his family. He's had a hell of a time."

"If it weren't about his 'stead, what were it?"

"Doc sent his wife to the asylum. Said she was insane. She had a tough time, but she wasn't crazy. She needed time to adjust to the awful things that happened. Doc wanted to help Deast get Sutton's entry, and that explains why the conspirators wanted Sutton's wife in the asylum. That much I know."

"That's a lot, but killin's a lot too."

"I told you; don't know there's a killing. Anyway, there was more. There was more."

"How much of this is goin' in yer paper?"

"None of it, Mr. Newton. None of it until you tell all this to the U.S. Attorney. Then all of it, sir. All of it, and the courts can decide."

"Got nothin' good to say about courts, sir. I read how they treat a rich man; know how they treat a poor one."

"It's the way. Only hope out here, sir, is law. It's the only hope."

"You got more trust in it than I do."

Newton picked up his hat and pushed it over his flowing white hair.

"You go to the U.S. Attorney, Mr. Newton. Go."

"I'll be thinkin' of it," he said. "Might want to talk again." He rose to leave, then paused.

"Can you spare me a dollar for a meal and a room?"

Widlund found a coin in his pocket and handed it to Newton.

"Stay in touch."

36

Almy and Mildred

IF ALMY had any comfort during these days, it was with Mildred. She enjoyed the order of her aunt's home. The furniture, the draperies, the doilies on the tables, the knick-knacks were to her like furnishings in a doll house. At the hut, she had only her imagination and her books to provide ideas. At Aunt Mildred's she had real things.

She especially loved the kitchen. Her aunt prepared the meals, made pies, and chatted happily. As she went along, she hummed constantly, as if keeping time to her thoughts. Almy could not recognize any melody. Instead, her aunt's sounds were more like rhythmic grunts.

Mildred found chores for Almy. She shared recipes, showed her how to prepare vegetables, prepare marinades for meats, roll crusts, and make coffee and tea. Their daily trips to market were punctuated with stops for conversation and cheerful greetings.

In the afternoons, Almy could sit on the porch or in the shade of the young cottonwood in the yard and read books from the library. With the companionship of a trusted relative, she relaxed, gained weight, and began to feel trust. Her nightmares continued, but with less intensity, and she often was able to get back to sleep instead of lying awake for the rest of the night, as she had done at the hut. She knew her father was in jail, and she knew why. She told Mildred that her Pa should not be alone. She said she should be there with him.

"You should be here with us, dear," Mildred said. "We will be strong as we've had to be all along."

"But he's not to blame."

"I know, child."

Mildred let these conversations pass. She could see no benefit to Almy in probing. She believed that her care in the matter was to help the girl find a bearing. She had seen her sister die in a blizzard. She had seen her mother disappear into an unreal world, and she had listened to her mother's confused talk. Now her mother was in an asylum and her father in jail, charged with murder. There was no need to add to the girl's worries. She needed a stable, loving atmosphere, and Mildred would do her best to provide it.

One morning after Charles had gone to the office, Almy was drying the dishes and putting them in the cupboard when she turned to her aunt and asked if they could talk.

"It's about Pa," she said.

Mildred stopped what she was doing and invited Almy to sit at the table. The kitchen door was wide open, and the screen held back a buzz of flies. The breeze was light and warm, and a pair of lark buntings chirped from the fence post. They settled into the narrow chairs and squared so their knees touched.

"What is it, Sweetheart?"

"Pa killed Doc," she said softly.

Mildred reached for the girl's hands and held them on her knees. Her hair was tied with a scarf, and her white apron was neatly draped over her blue dress. She leaned forward and looked at her niece tenderly.

"You don't have to tell me about this, dear."

"I saw him. He wouldn't stop choking him. Out by the barn."

"Sweetheart, please. You don't have to ..."

"Auntie ... I'm afraid."

"Of course you are. You are here now, and it's over."

"Pa will hang, won't he?"

Mildred couldn't answer. Nobody could prove Doc was even dead, let alone murdered. They would have to drop charges against Sutton, in time anyway.

"You don't have to say anything more, Almy. Nothing. Just let it be."

"The sheriff tricked me."

"What did you say to the sheriff?"

"He said Pa killed Doc, but I didn't say anything. Only that Doc was bad. He was bad!"

She cried, low sobs at first and when Mildred pulled her close, she stood with her head on her aunt's shoulder the tears broke and her cries became a low wail.

"We buried him in the Hills," she said, almost in a scream.

"You buried him?"

"Yes!" she screamed.

"You ... you were there, Sweetheart?"

"Me and Pa and Mr. Dimon. We put him in the sand and covered it over."

Mildred knew she shouldn't press on, but she did.

"Where?"

"Out in the hills. Some place Mr. Dimon knew about. We drug him out there and buried him."

She hugged the girl again and held her tight. She did not know what to say or do. Almy pushed away gently and looked at Mildred's face and could see the worry there.

"What are we going to do, Auntie? Pa's going to hang."

"Shhh. Not a word. Not a word."

<u>37</u>

Sutton tried for murder

THE MURDER trial of Will Sutton was well along before Jason Buck called Charles Widlund. Like any good lawyer, he knew how Widlund would answer his questions. His objective was to substantiate for the jury that Sutton stayed at the Widlund home a few days prior to the doctor's disappearance and that Sutton intended to have the doctor amputate his fingers.

Buck had personal interest in the outcome of the trial. The doctor was his friend. The two were partners in Deast Land and Cattle Co. And Sutton's claim was all but theirs once the settler was in prison. With Sutton's wife in the asylum and his daughter too young to manage the claim by herself, the Sutton claim would soon be in the public domain again. All Buck and Deast would need to do was file an objection to entry once Sutton had "abandoned" it for more than six months. The law gave first option on an abandoned claim to the person or persons who informed the government of the abandonment. It was the way the law was written.

Buck had deposed Widlund. In the deposition, Buck had asked Widlund if he thought his brother-in-law killed the doctor, and Widlund said he didn't think Sutton could hurt a flea. He said Sutton was a man who had suffered much, but he wasn't a violent man. Buck needed no more than this testimony.

He had deliberated quite some time about whether to put the girl on the stand. He was present when she implicated her father but asking a child to testify could backfire. Jury members might sympathize too much with the girl. Asking her for testimony that could implicate her own father was risky, so Buck decided against it. Buck knew, too, that Widlund thought the doctor was in cahoots with Deast and that the two of them wanted Sutton's claim. There would be no way to confirm that because Buck and Doc Bronson had covered their tracks well, including their interest in Deast Land and Cattle, which was held in the name of a dummy holding company they had established very early on. That meant that Widlund's suspicions, if Buck could goad him into disclosing them, would only further substantiate a motive for Sutton to be rid of the doctor.

Buck had not asked Widlund about Almy, because he had no knowledge of any impropriety. He had heard rumors of Doc's perverted interest in women, and he had himself wondered why the doctor never married or showed any normal interest in the opposite sex. He left that topic alone; he didn't care to know. Widlund volunteered nothing. Once he was sworn, Buck proceeded as he planned.

He asked him where Sutton's daughter Almy was at present, and Widlund explained that the girl was in the care of him and his wife.

"And, Mr. Widlund, can you tell us where Mr. Sutton's wife is?"

"She is in Hastings, Nebraska."

"Why is she there and not here?"

"She was committed to the insane asylum there."

"She is insane?"

"The Insanity Board said she is. You know that Mr. Buck, because you are on the Insanity Board."

"And was Will Sutton relieved that his wife was committed?"

"No, sir. He did not believe his wife was insane. He was not relieved at all."

"Was he angry?"

"Will does not show his emotions, sir. I believe it posed a hardship for him."

"So, he did not agree with the board's decision?"

"He did not, sir."

Buck felt confident that the questioning was going well for him. A motive was now clearly established. He told the judge he had no further questions, and Sutton's attorney was anxious to get Widlund off the stand. He asked Widlund where Almy was, and Widlund explained that the girl had been in the custody of himself and his wife. With that, Sutton's attorney dismissed Widlund.

Buck then called David Dimon. With Dimon he expected to accomplish two things. First Dimon could collaborate Sutton's motive. Second, and more importantly, he could establish that Dimon was the last person to see Doc Bronson alive, and that the doctor was headed to the Sutton homestead when Dimon saw him.

At the same time, he was not confident in Dimon. He knew him to be fiery and unpredictable, the worst kind of witness. He knew Dimon had run-ins with Deast, hated him, and disliked the doctor, too. But Dimon, in his deposition, testified that he met Doc Bronson on the road, and the doctor told Dimon he was on his way to Sutton's place. Without a body to confirm death and apparent homicide, Buck badly needed Dimon's testimony, even if it came with risks.

He was feeling more comfortable as the testimony progressed. Dimon confirmed all that he had said in the deposition.

"Did you see Doc Bronson at any time after your encounter with him on the road from Rackett?"

Dimon hesitated. Buck expected a quick reply in the negative. Dimon ran his fingers through his thin hair. He shifted in his chair. He was uneasy.

"Mr. Dimon ...?" Buck said.

"Oh. Sorry. What was it you asked?"

"Did you see Doc Bronson after you encountered him on the road to the Sutton entry?"

"Yes."

The courtroom silenced. The county attorney didn't know what to ask next, because he was not sure of the answer.

The judge waited long then he spoke. "Mr. Buck ... any further questions?"

"Ah ... yes, your honor. Mr. Dimon where did you see the doctor?"

"I saw 'im dead."

"You saw him dead?"

"Yessir. Lyin' dead in the road. Deader'n a door nail."

38

Trouble for Deast

"I SEE," Elias Hunter said. "You had orders from Rutherford Deast to kill Rootes Jackson? What about David Dimon?"

"He wanted Dimon too scairt to stay on with his 'stead. Dimon knew the black man, so we went for his place. Forced him to take us to Jackson."

Frosty Newton told Hunter the same story he told Widlund.

"What happened to Dimon?"

"I let 'im go. Didn't make sense to me, and two men dead in the sand already. Had enough."

"And now you're telling this to me because you want Deast to go to jail."

"Don't care what happens to 'im. Right is right, ain't it?"

Hunter studied the man. He was either a damned fool or had an uncommonly high-minded view of prairie justice. The people out here were driven by something at times hard to fathom. He and Ruhoff were in this god-forsaken part of the world to help establish law and order and to protect government land. That he could understand, if barely. As for this man Frosty Newton, Hunter found it hard to think a man would jeopardize his own neck for some hope of justice when he could just as easily disappear into the hills of Oklahoma or the plains of Texas.

"You are willing to testify before a court of law to this?"

"I expect some protection, naturally. Spent enough time breakin' rocks."

"That can be arranged. You must tell us everything you know. Everything. There cannot be any holes to your story."

"Nossir."

"This case is in federal court, you know?" "So?"

"That means it will be in Omaha. You will go back there. You will be indicted, and in return for your testimony against Deast, you will be granted immunity."

"How long this gonna take?"

"Can't say. Besides, you don't have any choice."

39

More news for the *Tribune*

AS HE HOPED, Widlund had what he needed to add to the dispatches from Omaha. The *Bee* and the *World-Herald* covered the Deast trial for their daily editions, and Widlund could summarize for his weekly. He wrote quickly and easily, drawing on the background he had from the depositions, the court proceedings, and all of it supported by his interview with Newton.

The two stories -- Sutton murder trial and the Deast criminal case -- dominated talk in Rackett. In the Sutton trial, a witness had said Doc Bronson's body was found on the south road. Now they were setting out to find the body and figure out how he died. But the county attorney's name had come up in the Deast case, too. So far, no indictments against him had been handed up, but folks speculated the Sutton case might be delayed for some time. The news hit the streets and folks in Rackett quickly parted with their nickels for copies. Did ya, hear? The best-known and richest cattle and land operation in the area was under indictment again! Not just the fencing, either. The federal government says Deast himself is implicated in acts of intimidation and conspiracy to defraud the 'steaders! Government says a black man from down toward Oshkosh been shot by one of Deast's men! Buck might be involved. Bronson, too! Looking for

Doc's body, too, but haven't found it! For once, Widlund thought with satisfaction, the newspaper is getting more attention than Ruthie Kremlacek.

40

The story at home

BETWEEN conversations with her husband, the gossip around town, and the stories in the newspaper, Mildred had a good idea of what was going on.

Dimon's testimony was not the same as Almy's story. Mildred did not suspect the child of fabricating any of it; her story poured out too easily, like water from a broken dam. Mildred didn't know Dimon. Maybe he just forgot. Not likely. He was lying.

Almy wondered if something was on Mildred's mind. As they cleared the table, Mildred hummed away as usual, saying nothing. The girl tried once to ask, but Mildred only brushed her off and went about her work. When the kitchen was tidy, Mildred suggested that Almy find a book and read in her room. The girl thought it odd but wanted to read anyway and seized the opportunity. In their parlor, Mildred sat at the edge of her chair as Widlund read through his newspapers.

"There's something you must know."

The tone wasn't lost on him. He put his papers down.

"She knows where he's buried. She helped. She was with Will and Dimon."

41

The exhumation

THE PROCESSION of buggies and riders went south from Rackett early on an August morning. By eight o'clock the sun coated the prairie in golden light and the grasses listed languidly on the hills. Collected heat from yesterday's blistering sun released skyward from the miles and miles of sand, distorting the vista with curious waves from the top of the hill.

Despite its grim objective, the voyage was pleasant. With its absence of trees, the landscape seemed to stretch before the travelers without end. The immensity of the Sand Hills, covering some 19,000 square miles, inspired awe, even to those souls who met its hardship head on while attempting to live in its cruel grasp. As in winter, the Hills in summer are alternately majestic and daunting, and this morning was so peaceful and warm that the riders could not resist commenting. But summer days could be unbearably hot and humid, with winds driving discomfort deep into one's soul. The procession seemed aware that the moment was uncommon and should be savored.

Dimon rode near the front with Sheriff Brier at his side. Behind were the twelve jury members, some on horseback, others in buggies. The county attorney and Sutton's attorney for the defense followed. Judge Bedington had instructed everyone to be silent on the trip; he wanted no influence on the jurors, especially from the attorneys. Of course, that was impossible.

The procession came to the top of the hill, and as the horses were reined to a halt, the chatter commenced. Judge Bedington let it go, himself enjoying the moment. He eventually recognized his duty and motioned the people to be attentive, and the voices yielded to the whistling breeze. Dimon reined his horse to a stop, and one by one the members of the entourage circled.

"This is the place?" said the judge.

"Not here. Down, yonder," and Dimon pointed west.

He took the lead, but the buggies rebelled. Sheriff Brier called everyone to a halt, and after a brief discussion it was decided that only horses would go on. Some of the people doubled up on horseback, and others walked. The wind stiffened as they descended the hill and made the turn to the right, up the draw and into the valley.

They had gone on this way for a half hour when Dimon reined his horse and sat.

"I think maybe it's this way," he said.

His uncertainty was not lost on the group, and glances were exchanged, betraying their doubts.

"You think? You don't know where you buried this man?" said the judge.

Dimon felt the doubts and his eyes darted from the accusing judge to the areas that lay in front of the procession. He carefully scanned the valley, looking for the scant trail. He was confused.

He said, "We musta missed the turn."

He reined his horse around and backtracked, and as he passed the entourage behind him, they gave him curious looks. He hadn't made a convincing witness; his story of the body on the road already had been doubted by some of the jurors. Now as he hesitated in this spot to which he had led them, they began to wonder if the old man was a bit crazy.

They followed him back toward the road, but they hadn't gone long when he stopped to examine the draw to his right. The entourage pulled up behind him, then he pointed west again, and they began again.

This time Dimon seemed sure of himself. They went on, and he stopped again.

"Thought it was down here," he said.

"Mr. Dimon. You are leading us all over the place," the judge said. "Do you know where we are going?"

The old man motioned them on, and they followed again. This time he turned them left to the south and into the blazing sun. Then he pulled up again and stopped. He pointed west again, and the group went that way into another draw. When the chokecherries came into view, Dimon yelled. "Here! Here! This way!"

He led them on. Then he pulled up and dismounted, the others gathered in a tight group, waiting. He wandered around, his head down as if a diviner for water, looking for the place. He kicked in the sand and around in the grass, and again seemed befuddled.

"Here! Dig here."

The sheriff dismounted and took the short-handled shovel lashed to his saddle. He asked Dimon where, and the old man pointed to a soft place in the sand. When he started to dig, Dimon changed his mind, paced a few steps away and said here. The sheriff started again, and again, Dimon changed his mind.

As the summer sun Their impatience grew. Dimon tried one last time, and the sheriff dug. This time Dimon didn't call him off. The area didn't look much disturbed, but Dimon seemed sure of himself this time. The sheriff dug a trench, oriented north and south, as Dimon told him.

The trench grew in depth and length, but nothing showed. Dimon asked him to move to the east, and the sheriff widened the trench in that direction. When that turned up nothing, Dimon suggested they extend the trench to the north, and the sheriff dug.

"Here's something," he said with clear lack of enthusiasm. He dug some more than yelled out," My god!"

The judge came around, and Dimon said, "There. I told ya judge. This right here where I buried 'im."

The sheriff bent to his knees and with his hands uncovered the shoulders of a man. He cleared away more dirt and found the decaying neck and then the head.

The skull was visible now, but the ears were gnawed away by the creatures in the sand. The jurors stood around the open grave.

"Good god!" Dimon said.

Silence came over the crowd. The wind rose and the hot air stirred the chokecherries, whipping them loudly. A towering cumulus cloud rolled over, and the sunlight was blocked.

The jurors stared into the hole and at the body which lay face down. The hair remained, and everyone knew there was no Doc Bronson here, just the decayed body of a man who had black skin.

42

Life goes on

SUTTON WAS released and the murder charge dropped. Without a body to prove Bronson was even dead, there was no case. Had someone witnessed the crime or seen the body disposed of, the county might have had a circumstantial case. Apart from Dimon, there was no witness. A few jurors thought the old man was crazy anyway -- 'tetched' as one of the jurors put it.

The body of the black man they discovered in a shallow grave must have been the homesteader from near Oshkosh. When they asked around, no one could say they'd seen Rootes Jackson for quite some time. He might have gone south to Texas. Couldn't tell by his face; it was blown off, and his neck severed, probably throat slit. The sheriff puzzled over it but decided to cover the body with sand and forget it.

Sutton and Almy resumed life at the soddie. So little work had been done during the growing season that fall seemed relaxed but worrisome. Sutton built fence on the southwest quarter of his section, the part that bordered Deast's section purchased from Tomppert for a hundred dollars. A shack had been erected, and Deast had a man staying there during the warm months, enough to satisfy the letter of the Kincaid law. Deast was in jail, but the government had not yet reversed his claim to the fraudulent entries. Sutton could not be sure who his neighbor would be, but in any event, he intended to complete a barbed wire fence along the property line.

With his sulky, he cut bottom hay, but the yield was so skimpy it almost wasn't worth the effort. Still, he raked it and hauled it to the loft; it would help feed his team during the coming winter months.

With Mildred and Charles, he signed the letter appealing Maddie's commitment. Hunter, feeling some gratitude for Widlund's help in building a case against Deast, made a case for Maddie's release with Interior Secretary Hitchcock. To his surprise, Hitchcock was so incensed (and fearful for his job because the president was not happy with the light sentences Deast had received the first time around) that he forwarded specifics of Maddie's case to Roosevelt himself. When the director at the Hastings asylum received a letter from the president suggesting that he re-examine the competency of one Maddie Sutton, the wheels suddenly turned. The woman was perfectly fit to re-enter society, the director said.

The letter arrived at Widlund's office on a warm Friday in September. The day after publication day was usually quiet, even though there were mountains of work to do. When he saw who the letter was from, he ripped it open quickly then raced home to share the news with Mildred.

"In a week!" she said.

Maddie's arrival was celebrated with dinner at the soddie. Charles and Mildred rode out, and a breezy early autumn day greeted them. They brought beef to roast and pies made with early-autumn apples.

Jay and Elsie Adams came from their homestead with mountains of prepared food, and a table as well, anticipating that the Suttons would not have room for every person. Sutton and Jay pulled the table from inside the hut to the outdoors, and they nestled the two tables close. The Adams' horses were unhitched, and Sutton and Widlund backed up the top buggy so it could serve as a sideboard.

Except for the anticipation of Maddie's new presence, the picnic was like many the Sand Hills settlers had. Everyone's eyes were on Maddie. The collective goal was to welcome her and to brush aside as smoothly as possible the ordeal she had experienced. Mildred seemed to handle the job as a good sister would, helping, chatting, and keeping the conversation both pleasant and genuine. Maddie seemed to set everyone's mind at ease when she spoke easily of the beauty of the autumn afternoon.

"I am so happy to be in my home," she said.

"We are so happy to have you," Mildred said. Her smile was soft and sincere, surprisingly void of condescension.

Jay Adams rose from his seat at the foot of the table, and asked everyone to stand with him. As he usually did, he bowed his head and loudly proclaimed his gratitude to the good lord for the food they all were about to receive, the standard prayer that he recited each time he visited with a neighbor or at a picnic. His Christian faith was tolerated, and his evangelism accepted as if it were no less a part of the homestead fabric than the oaths sodbusters swore at their balky team or their broken plow. Amens echoed around the table, and the group sat again, as if choreographed dancers.

Maddie sat to Sutton's left. Her hair was pulled tight against her head, making her face seem thinner. Never more than slight anyway, she now seemed frail and drained of the strength that years of homestead work had given her. Her complexion, sallow from the three months she had been confined indoors, contrasted with Sutton's weathered face.

Almy sat across from her. She was bright with excitement. The prospect of having her mother home eclipsed her worry. With youthful resilience, she put away her sadness and embraced the joy she felt in the company of her family and friends. Her nightmares had stopped. No longer did she dream of the doctor's sneering face as he stalked her across the plains in half-moon light and howling winds. Nor did she see his expressionless dead eyes and his neck with the blackening puncture wounds. As if washed away in a spring rain, the horrors of her recent months began to fade.

"Almy, please pass the potatoes," Maddie said, and Almy almost jumped from her chair to comply. Her smile broadened as her blue eyes searched for meaning on her mother's face. When Maddie would smile, even faintly, Almy would beam, and her cheeks would flush red with joy. When Maddie spoke, Almy was rapt; every word her other uttered was precious to her.

Jay and Elsie were careful. They wanted only to be helpful. They spoke quietly and always with forced smiles intended to signal their understanding and warmth. Elsie divided her concern between Maddie and Almy. She watched the child and was buoyed by her enthusiasm. She felt deep bonds to the girl; in Maddie's absence they had become close. Almy could open up with Elsie, as she could with Mildred, and the comforting conversations were helpful in restoring the girl's normal development. Scars from her experiences were forming, and Elsie and Mildred seemed to know that no time would erase them all, but careful attention now to her needs could help her get past most of it.

Widlund had brought his new camera to the picnic. When the meal was finished, he ordered everyone to remain seated at the table while he arranged himself with his spanking new Brownie No. 2. He pressed the button and the lens folded out from its accordion bellows.

"Hold very still," he said as he took a deep breath and held it.

"No smiles! Hold still!"

The small camera rested in his hands and as gently as he could, he pressed the shutter lever. When they heard the click, they relaxed and chatted enthusiastically about the new cameras available through the Sears and Roebuck catalogue.

"Wait, everyone!" he said. "Let's have a picture of just the Suttons on their reunion day."

Sutton smoothed his mound of wavy hair with both hands, and Maddie adjusted her dress. Almy, happy at the idea, beamed. Widlund arranged them so that Maddie and Sutton stood together, with Almy at her mother's side. Again, he ordered absolute stillness and no smiles. Sutton let his arms hang loosely with his palms on the thighs of his pants. Widlund adjusted everyone until the afternoon sunlight would be on their faces, and the shadows of their features were distinct.

When Widlund had finished his portrait, Maddie reached for Sutton's hands and held them gently so she could examine them.

"They're almost healed, Will," she said. "It must have been so painful."

Almy winced at the memory, and her joy suddenly turned to anguish. She turned away and ran to the pond hiding her tears and sobs.

Jay said, "Oh my, we must have upset her."

Elsie said, "There, there" in the direction of Maddie.

Mildred went after Almy and they chatted quietly in the distance. Maddie's first inclination was to go with Mildred, but she held. Soon, Mildred returned with the girl, and she seemed to have composed herself.

Widlund sat at the table with the camera in front of him and fiddled with it as though repairing something. The moment soon drifted away and was forgotten. No one paid Widlund any mind, and he said nothing at all.

43

Upon reflection

THE MAIL from Eastman Kodak arrived a few weeks later. Widlund opened the package and removed the prints. He leafed through them quickly, photos of the picnic, the group, one photo of the sod hut taken from the hill to its north, and one of Mildred taken just after he loaded the film before they left Rackett. He was captivated by the photo of the Suttons.

Will, Maddie and Almy had followed his instructions and kept very still, no smiles or other change in expressions, chiseled like statues. He turned the print over and wrote September 16, 1907. He followed suit with the other prints.

It was a fine Saturday afternoon in October, and the throes of autumn and the hints of winter were around him on the porch. As he pushed his rocking chair back from the side table, an easy gust whipped the prints away. He gathered them quickly as Mildred opened the screen door, talking as she went inside.

"We may have a still day in summer or winter or fall or spring, but then comes a wind," she said.

She returned with cups of hot tea and put them on the table.

"Brrr . . . it's too chilly for me," she said. "I need a wrap."

She went quickly into the house and returned with a shawl crocheted with thick yarns of orange, green and brown, which she snugged around her shoulders. Of course, she had a book, too. She settled into the other rocker and sipped her tea before opening the book. She snugged the wrap and settled. Widlund glanced her way casually.

"That's new, isn't it?

"Maddie made it while she was away."

"What are you devouring," Widlund asked.

"Devouring?"

"The book. What is it?"

"I'm getting very philosophical. It's because of the season, I suspect. Have you ever thought about how, this time of year, all the energy seems to run out? I think how the plants bud then bloom, then grow and flourish," she paused. "Now they wither like a lamp running low on fuel."

Widlund grunted and continued to look into the eyes of the Suttons. His pictures were very sharp. The combination of perfect light and the stoic stillness of his subjects produced near-perfect images. He felt proud, as if the camera had been his personal invention. The pictures brought him deep satisfaction. Photography was a new skill he was acquiring. He read as much as he could find about the new technology. He was especially interested, of course, in how it would apply to his newspaper.

He studied Will's eyes. The halftones beneath them defined the folds. He counted four of them, very distinct beneath his right eye, but only three beneath the left. To the outside edge of each eye was a deep crease etched by countless grins. There was no color in the photograph, only variations in black and white. Widlund knew Will's eyes to be blue, but here for the historical record they were light grey. Sutton had focused his gaze slightly to the left of Widlund's camera, and that pose gave the impression that he had just been asked a question by another person, or that someone he knew had just walked by.

His brother-in-law's nose, Widlund knew, was prominent and pointed, but in the photo, with Sutton mostly squared to the camera, there was nothing more than the deep creases of his cheeks to suggest how substantial it was. His ears protruded only slightly from his head, and his hair had been trimmed roughly above them in a choppy taper. Almost precisely above the corner of his left eye, the ample brown hair was parted and rose like hills above a valley.

Most notably to Widlund was the man's square chin. Combined with the craggy features, clear eyes, and prominent nose, the chin presented a face entirely consistent with Widlund's understanding of his brother-in-law. Strong. Indomitable. Indefatigable. Nearly all the years of experience Widlund had with Sutton supported these adjectives. There was no exaggeration.

He was pleased with the light on Maddie's hair. She had parted her auburn locks dead center at her symmetrical forehead and pulled them tight then held them in place with pins. To diminish her small but protruding ears, she combed the sides in tufts above each of them, pinned them at her neck, and then with Almy's help braided them snugly. The sun reflected from the top of her head like a full moon above her dark eyes. She gazed intently in the opposite direction of Sutton, to the right of the camera and adopted a frozen stare, her interpretation of Widlund's instruction to hold perfectly still. Her lips, slightly parted, hid her crooked teeth. Her cheeks were sunken and her skin pale, so smooth that the camera captured only white, no definition at all of a single crease at her eyes, on her cheeks, or on her forehead. Her thin nose was defined only by her small nostrils, like dots on a porcelain plate.

Widlund was lost in the image. He recognized the facial similarities to Mildred, but he was absorbed in the thought of Maddie's ordeal. There was a freshness to her face. He thought it was not accurate, that the film must have somehow captured the light and transfigured it in an untrue representation. His mind told him there should be wrinkles from sadness and despair, from loss and mourning. But the image presented none of that. He had thought she would never recover, but now as he sat and pondered his remarkable image, he recognized that it presented serenity, not despair, understanding and not confusion, forgiveness and not anger.

The image of Almy troubled him. It wasn't disappointment that he felt, but he wished for more clarity. Evidently, she had moved her eyes as the shutter released, and although her facial features were otherwise clear, her eyes were ill-defined splatters of gray and black. If he were a portrait artist, he thought, he would have devoted much care to painting the child's eyes. He would have preferred to suggest wonder and excitement, perhaps a cautious openness, as Vermeer did with his girl. He knew most of what she experienced, and she carried her secret bravely. He remembered that her thirteenth birthday was just days away, on October 20th, and he wished he could see more deeply into her being, because he cared for her as if she were his own daughter, and he worried for her future.

"You're deep in thought," Mildred said.

He felt as if he'd been shaken from sleep.

"I'm looking at these pictures, Mildred," he said. "They turned out well, didn't they?"

"You have a rare talent there, Mr. Widlund," she said with a broad smile.

He rocked gently, and she sipped her tea, complaining that it had gotten too cool.

"You're absorbed with your photographs, and I'm enjoying my book. We've forgotten our tea," she said.

"I'm wondering," he said, " ... Is it ever right to intervene in the process of law? I mean, what if the law, if it played out properly, would have an outcome that would not square with the real evil done?"

She placed her book on her lap and looked at him. It was clear he was serious. The question, as she repeated it in her mind, was vague. But she could tell he intended a precise answer.

"I do think I'm going to need more information if you intend me to answer."

"I have hoped for lawfulness to arrive in our community, but I'm afraid it's slow coming."

"Yes, but it is arriving. European peoples have been in this wild country only a few decades. We have a sheriff and a judge, and Nebraska has a fine court system. We even have our own newspaper and an editor with a proper sense of justice."

She smiled and studied his face. He did not acknowledge her compliment.

"I wonder if I did the right thing, with the graves, mixing them ... " he said.

He said more but the sentence was lost in a whistling gust. The prints scattered. He and Mildred scrambled to gather them, but another gust sent the remaining ones off again, and they chased after them like children in the schoolyard.

"How many do you have?" he said. "Three!"

"I have four. There's one missing." They searched the bushes downwind.

"Here it is," Mildred said. "It's the one of the three of them. I'm afraid there's a little damage."

He took the photograph and turned it. The wind had thrown it into a rose bush and punctured it near the corner.

"It's small. Just a hole."

He handed the photograph to her, and she admired it.

"They look so beautiful. After all they've been through."

"Almy ... I worry about the girl."

"She's young, Charles. I worry, too, but I think she'll be fine. They love her so."

"She's seen a lot."

"I think she will recover. Bad things can be forgotten. It's the way we do."

"She saw what her father did. I worry about the gruesome things she saw. The burial ..."

"Charles, please. If she hadn't told me, you wouldn't have known what to do."

"I don't think she could have taken any more. She didn't need to see her father in jail."

"Well, he was acquitted. They will never find the body."

"The right body, with the right head."

"Thanks to Crazy Dimon."

"Crazy Dimon. Crazy like a fox. He put an end to that sad story, didn't he?"

"He led that jury there."

"He knew what they'd find. It was a gruesome deed, Mildred. Dimon and the white-haired man knew where both bodies lay. Switching the heads seemed the only answer."

"You were right to suggest it. It's a shame for that black settler. People say he was very nice. It's a shame he lay in the same sand as the doctor."

"Part of him."

"At least they know where he's buried. No one ever will know where the doc is, and he's so close by."

"They've erected a nice cross and put some flowers for Mr. Jackson. Ruthie Kremlacek told me."

"The voice of Rackett."

"She does like to gossip."

"Every town needs one," Widlund said.

They rocked quietly. The wind settled, and the autumn air turned cool. The sun drifted slowly down. Soon it would be too cold to remain outside, and they would go in.

ACKNOWLEDGEMENTS AND NOTES

"Sandhills" and "Sand Hills" are alternate names. Locals tend to use the former. The author has chosen to use the latter for no important reason.

The Denver Public Library and its reference and western history research staff are friendly, patient, and knowledgeable assistants in research.

In Oshkosh, Nebraska, there are dedicated stewards of that region's heritage, especially Verna Bairn, who will brave any weather to open either of the two Garden County museums for visitors, and County Clerk and Recorder Teresa McKeeman, who keeps records and shares them with interest.

Stephen R. Jones of Boulder, Colorado, has written a delightful book called "The Last Prairie, a Sandhills Journal." His descriptions of the wildlife, grasses, and birds are masterful. He beautifully relates the story of Lost Chokecherry Valley, as told by Maria Sandoz. Lost Chokecherry Valley hasn't been precisely located, although there are several ideas about where it might have been. It is used fictitiously in this book. Both Mr. Jones and I have snapped photos of the Sand Hills, and it is testimony to the country out there that the photos are so similar.

Jay and Elsie Adams, the author's grandparents, filed for a Kincaid in 1912, soon after the act was revised to require only three years to prove up. They moved there when the author's mother was an infant. They didn't have easy times, but theirs was not the experience of the fictional characters the author created. With the determination of Paul and the patience of Job, the authors grandparents proved up, and their patent was mailed to their post office box in the now-gone town of Rackett, Nebraska, in 1916.

The Brothers Grimm inspired the image of a poor mother beating down the extended hand of her buried child.

William Shakespeare, in his play Othello, thought of including a white handkerchief embroidered with strawberries as a literary device to symbolize jealousy and betrayal. Here it is evidentiary and a symbol of defiled purity.

A wonderful man named JB Winsor, a former newspaperman who now writes novels and short stories, edited early versions of the novel, and provided many valuable suggestions.

Jennifer Disposti has worked with horses all her life and knows them well. She helped the author describe how horses can sense and react to imminent weather changes.

Early readers offered many valuable suggestions and helped catch errors. Among them are my children, Dawn Sand, Sarah Rogers, Tim Stewart, and Jude Stewart. Meg Knox, Jane Allen, Jan Burton, Margaret Thomas, Rebecca Poth, Pat Cummings, Rick Scheideman, Caroline Hoyt, Tom Hoyt, Dan Sher, Don Johnson, and Dean Colby helped discover some of the many typographical errors that somehow sneaked into early versions of the manuscript. Attentive readers surely have spotted more.

The author's coffee group friends, Jack Thompson, John Winsor, Stewart Hoover, Mike Maloy, Alan Rudy, Lewis House, Paul Bauman, Andy Skumanich, Fred Ris, and John Sadler expressed their interest and offered their encouragement.

The author's partner, Becky Roser, generously offered ideas, caught typos, and listened and listened and listened as a good friend and fellow life traveler alone can do.

www.ingramcontent.com/pod-product-compliance
Lightning Source LLC
Chambersburg PA
CBHW070452120726
47910CB00003B/1017